'You're a

'Why not?'

'Well. . .' G ... ner wayward thoughts, she blurted out, 'If you're a doctor, why did your friend come to me? Surely you should have seen that she needed professional help? And understood that a doctor's appointment about childhood sniffles with two juveniles erupting around the place wasn't going to be the answer! And you accuse *me* of unprofessional conduct!'

Dear Reader

Nature gets its own back this month! Stella Whitelaw's DELUGE takes us to the dangerous waters of the North Sea, and Meredith Webber's WHISPER IN THE HEART includes a terrifying bush fire! There's water in HEARTS AT SEA by Clare Lavenham, following a cruise ship, but STILL WATERS—despite the title!—by Kathleen Farrell brings us to earth in Edinburgh. All good stuff for you to enjoy.

The Editor

!!!STOP PRESS!!! If you enjoy reading these medical books, have you ever thought of writing one? We are always looking for new writers for LOVE ON CALL, and want to hear from you. Send for the guidelines, with SAE, and start writing!

Having pursued many careers—from schoolteaching to pig farming—with varying degrees of success and plenty of enjoyment, **Meredith Webber** seized on the arrival of a computer in her house as an excuse to turn to what had always been a secret urge—writing. As she had more doctors and nurses in the family than any other professional people, the medical romance seemed the way to go! Meredith lives on the Gold Coast of Queensland, with her husband and teenage son.

Recent titles by the same author:

A TESTING TIME
HEALING LOVE

WHISPER IN THE HEART

BY

MEREDITH WEBBER

MILLS & BOON

MILLS & BOON LIMITED
ETON HOUSE, 18–24 PARADISE ROAD
RICHMOND, SURREY, TW9 1SR

All the characters in this book have no existence outside the imagination of the Author, and have no relation whatsoever to anyone bearing the same name or names. They are not even distantly inspired by any individual known or unknown to the Author, and all the incidents are pure invention.

First published in Great Britain 1994 by Mills & Boon Limited

This edition 1994

ISBN 0 263 78759 1

Set in 10 on 11 pt Linotron Times
03-9409-56586

Typeset in Great Britain by Centracet, Cambridge
Made and printed in Great Britain

CHAPTER ONE

'Is Dr Wainwright still here?' the man asked rudely, bounding up the stairs towards Gemma as she pulled the door of the surgery shut behind her.

Go away! she wanted to yell, but instead she said quietly, 'I'm Dr Wainwright. Is it urgent or could you come back tomorrow?' Her bag slid to the ground and she folded her arms defensively across her chest. Would he hear the aching tiredness she felt reflected in her voice?

'You're the only Dr Wainwright in this practice?' he demanded with an incredulity that would have been amusing if she hadn't heard the reaction countless times in the past.

'I'm the only doctor in this practice, and in this town,' she told him tartly. She would have liked to add, So if you need a doctor you're stuck with me, but inbred good manners—and the towering height and impressive bulk of the stranger—held her tongue still.

'You don't look old enough to be out of school let alone through medicine,' he muttered.

She felt the first stirring of resentment that comments about her appearance still provoked, although she understood why people who did not know her would be surprised and somewhat wary. Slightly built, with long, honey-coloured hair pulled back from a thin, pointed face—elfin, her mother said kindly, but she knew childlike was probably a more apt description—she appeared to be little more than a teenager. Especially at a time like this, when exhaustion from an interrupted night's sleep and a long, tiring day shrank her skin on to her bones, making her appear gaunt, and even smaller.

'Is it urgent?' she repeated, wishing this critical stranger would go away and let her leave. She had a house-call to do before she could contemplate ending her day's work with a quick meal, a long bath and the welcome comfort of her bed.

'No! Yes!'

He seemed angry and confused and she looked at him properly for the first time, seeking some clue to his problem in the physical appearance of the man. He appeared healthy enough—aggressively so—judging from the restrained energy that flowed from his body.

He was tall, his eyes on a level with hers although he had stopped, and now stood, two steps below the veranda. His hair was dark, and waved untidily back from a broad, strong forehead. His eyes, shadowed in the evening twilight, might be blue or grey, as they gleamed with a pale intensity that brown eyes rarely showed. His nose, like the broad shoulders and solid chest, suggested football in his past, for its classic straightness was marred by a slight inclination to the left, as if it had been pushed to one side so often it had decided to stay there.

'Did you see a young mother with twin boys earlier this afternoon?' he asked abruptly, obviously still in doubt about her professional stature. She switched her mind from noses to medicine.

'Yes, I did,' she responded quickly as her interest was caught and held. 'Has the feverishness developed into something—have they come out in spots or a rash——?'

'No, they haven't!' he cut in crossly. 'Although I'd already told their mother they were probably sickening for something. There was no need for her to drag them down here, but, as she did, she deserved to be treated with professional respect!'

Even in the fading light she could see his brow creasing into a fierce frown and feel a build-up of anger emanating from him, throbbing through the air towards her.

'You might be qualified as a doctor,' he stormed, emphasising the 'might' subtly enough to underline the doubt that still lingered in his mind, 'but unless you have five-year-old twin boys you're hardly qualified to pass judgement on their upbringing.'

'What are you talking about?' Gemma was flabbergasted by the man's words which seemed to hit her like sharp objects flung in the abandonment of irrational fury.

'I'm talking about your attitude towards that woman this afternoon! I'm talking about ethics, and unprofessional conduct, and overstepping the boundaries of your duties and——'

'Unprofessional conduct?' Gemma could not believe what she was hearing.

'Unprofessional conduct,' he reiterated firmly while the whole scene took on an air of unreality as Gemma's tired mind picked up the two words and turned them into a tuneless ditty. 'Presuming to tell a woman you've never met before how she should bring up her children. If that's not overstepping the bounds of proper conduct, I don't know what is!'

'Now stop right there!' Gemma's voice was cold and carefully controlled, but had any of the inhabitants of Grange Bay been passing they would have read the signs and beat a hasty retreat. It might only explode once every two years, but Gemma Wainwright's temper was a byword in the town, like old Jock Stapler's drinking bouts and Ma Kelly's home-made rissoles. They were the foundation of folklore, the birth of legends! Sad to say, there was not one local witness, late on this fine summer afternoon when Gemma's top blew again!

She planted her hands firmly on her hips and stepped towards her tormentor.

'I don't know who you are, mister, and I don't want to know, but don't stand here on *my* steps and tell me how to run my practice.' She stamped her small foot to emphasise the words. 'If your wife has any complaints, the number for the regional health authority is in the book. There won't be anyone there at this time of the night, and tomorrow will probably be someone's flexi-day, but she's welcome to keep trying, and to tell them exactly what she thinks of me.'

Gemma paused for breath, but the shadowy figure remained silent. She let her wrath continue to pour forth.

'And while she's on the phone, she might point out that, while one doctor is adequate for a town this size nine months of the year, when the population trebles at Christmas and Easter it is impossible to give every patient the time and consideration they think they deserve, and when people come in who simply need someone to listen to all their problems I may become a trifle short with them, particularly when their two little boys are wrecking my room and the woman has the temerity to reach into her handbag and settle back in the chair to enjoy a cigarette while she chats!'

Remembering the moment and the woman's shocked disbelief, Gemma's anger eased slightly, and she nearly smiled. Reaching across the desk, she had removed the cigarette from between the woman's lips, and returned it to the packet on the desk in one swift, easy movement. 'You'll be happier smoking outside,' she'd said, effectively ending the consultation! Behind her, the old skeleton she'd had from student days had crashed to the floor with a jangling clatter of bones, and one of the twins had yelped in pain.

Chaos had ensued, and she had finally ushered the three visitors out through the door, with the woman protesting volubly and the boys squabbling over the jelly beans she'd been foolish enough to bestow on them.

'If I remember rightly, the only judgement I passed was on her smoking in the same room as the boys,' Gemma told the stranger, her voice cold with the contempt she felt for parents who had such little concern for their children's health.

'You didn't tell her she was a poor excuse for a mother and that there was nothing wrong with the boys that a good hiding wouldn't cure?'

The accusation stunned Gemma into silence, cooling the flames of her anger. She thought back.

'I may have said that all children needed limits,' she answered slowly, 'but I think someone who is seeking attention as desperately as your wife is would probably exaggerate whatever was said to her.'

Regret crept into her voice. She should have made the time to listen to the woman instead of hustling her out of the door. The twins' feverish sniffles had been an excuse for the woman to visit the doctor, and, although she had half recognised that fact, she had not dealt sympathetically with her.

'. . .not my wife,' the man was saying, and Gemma forced her mind back to the present. 'She's a friend who's going through complicated marital problems at the moment. She's already suffered enough battering to her self-esteem! There is no excuse for speaking to her as you did.'

Bright flags of colour returned to Gemma's pale cheeks as the anger rekindled, but at that moment the pager in her pocket went off with a shrilling insistence.

The man reacted automatically, patting his pockets as if to find the electronic nuisance and silence it, but Gemma had removed hers and checked the telephone number it showed.

'You'll have to excuse me,' she said shortly, picking up her bag and moving towards the stairs.

'Aren't you going back into your office to phone that caller?'

She was staggered by his presumption and the disgust in his voice told her he wasn't finished with his complaints.

'If you would let me get down my own steps, I can answer it in person. It just so happens I would have been there ten minutes ago if I hadn't been held up by this pointless discussion of your friend's wounded ego.'

The word 'friend' had an unmistakable emphasis, and Gemma pushed past her unwelcome visitor and hurried down the steps.

Street-lamps cast soft pools of light across the pavement, but it wasn't until she bent to unlock the door of her car that she saw the deflated tyre.

'Just what I need!' she muttered in frustration, kicking at the offending rubber. A quick glance up and down the quiet street failed to reveal a friend who might come to her rescue.

'I'll change it for you.' It was her antagonist from the stairs. He'd followed her down and stood beside her, surveying the flattened tyre with a complacent ease. The offer was civil, but perceptibly cool in tone.

'I haven't time,' she retorted. 'That call meant they need me out at Orana. I'll go down into town and hope Grange Bay's one and only taxi is available.'

'I can take you wherever you need to go,' he offered, waving his hand towards a dark-coloured Range Rover parked behind her car. Gemma hesitated for an instant, but knew she couldn't refuse. The town's cab was probably busy ferrying visitors out to dinner.

The man seemed sane enough, she decided, glancing at him again. A bit over-protective of his girlfriend perhaps, but if she was divorcing her husband to marry him then he had a right to be apprehensive. She shrugged aside her doubts and nodded.

'I'd appreciate that,' she told him. 'If you drop me out there, I'll ring the garage and get them to fix the tyre, then their lad can come out and collect me later.'

He led the way back to his car, unlocked the passenger door, and reached out his hand to grasp her arm and help her up the high step into the vehicle. Her skin responded to his touch with a burning excitement and Gemma flinched, shocked by a reaction she could not understand.

'Which way?' He asked the question as he started the engine, and Gemma directed him back down the hill, through the town and out along the beach road.

Even in a car as roomy as this, she felt his presence as a physical force. It's because he's so large, she told herself, slanting her eyes towards him in the dim interior. His commanding masculinity crackled in the air like an electric current, alighting on her skin and sparking her nerve-endings to an acute awareness.

'Are you sure there's a house out there?' he asked, breaking into her erratic fancies as they passed the last straggle of houses on the edge of the little town.

'It's right at the end of the track,' she explained. They left the bitumen and bumped over the corrugated dirt road. 'One of the old farmhouses from the days when fishermen, timber-cutters and farmers first settled in this area, and Grange Bay was a quiet seaside town.'

'You resent the holiday people?'

His perception surprised her, and she thought for a moment before replying.

'Not entirely,' she admitted. 'Now the dairy farms are gone, the town needs the seasonal influx of people to keep it financially viable. We turn left here.'

Waving a hand towards the gate, Gemma looked ahead to the brightly lit old house, and decided that some explanations about Orana might be more appropriate than further discussion on the tourist problems of Grange Bay.

'This house is a respite care centre for children with disabilities. They come here throughout the year, but it's especially busy in school holidays. They enjoy a good time at the beach and their parents have a break from the added burden of rearing a child with a disability.'

'I've heard about respite services for elderly people,' her chauffeur said, obviously interested in what she was saying, 'but hadn't thought about the problems carers have with kids!'

'It's a great service,' Gemma enthused. 'The staff here can take up to five children at a time. Unfortunately, at the moment four of the five have chickenpox.' She sighed, remembering the hours she had spent here last night, helping to bathe feverish little bodies in Pinetarsal. 'If you think twin boys are a problem, you should try coping with three hyperactive kids with itching blisters all over them.'

As she spoke, they pulled up outside the gate that led into the enclosed yard, and she turned towards him, obscurely pleased that their earlier differences had been set aside.

His profile was etched against the lights of the house. His lips were well-defined, and showed a slight upward curve at the corners, as if they smiled a lot.

'Thank you very much for the lift,' she said quickly, dismayed by the path her tired mind was taking. 'I'm sorry if I offended your friend——' why couldn't she think of the woman's name? '—but it was unintentional, and I do think she needs professional counselling. Ordinary GPs can only do so much, you know,' she explained, not wanting him to leave with a bad impression of her. 'A good psychologist would be able to suggest ways for her to handle the things that are troubling her.'

Pain or guilt? she wondered, but couldn't possibly ask!

'I'll wait here and take you back to town,' he offered casually.

'That's not necessary,' Gemma told him, opening the door of the car as one of the helpers emerged on to the wide veranda of the low-set old house and peered out into the darkness beyond the lights. 'I'll arrange something. Thanks again!'

She dropped lightly to the ground and hurried inside, her mind already switching from the odd, unsettling encounter to the possible problems she might find in the house.

'Little Maggie had a full-blown seizure three-quarters of an hour ago,' Suzi greeted her as she hurried up into the house. 'We did what you'd showed us and then rang you to come out and check on her, but she's certainly come out of it.'

'I had a flat tyre,' Gemma explained, following the young woman through the old rambling house to Maggie's bedroom, where the pale little girl lay sleeping, watched over by an anxious young woman and a middle-aged man. Gemma noted the regular rhythmic breathing, then lifted one small hand to check Maggie's pulse. She felt the warmth immediately.

'She's probably caught the chickenpox as well,' she told the anxious carers gathered at the end of the bed as the little girl stirred and opened her eyes to gaze sleepily at her attendants. 'I'll check for an ear infection, and we'll get some liquid Panadol into her to keep her temperature down, but she's certainly out of the seizure.' She smiled at them. 'You've done well,' she assured them. 'I know it's not easy the first time.'

'I'll get the tepid water. I'm good at this now,' Ros replied, dashing out of the door, while Michael Dodds put a reassuring arm around his wife's shoulders and held her close.

'Suzi did it,' he explained, pride overtaking the strain in his voice. 'I was all prepared to panic and come rushing into town, but she knew exactly what to do.'

'I think twelve months as houseparents out here has taught you both to cope well with most emergencies. You do a great job,' she added sincerely, sliding her arm under the small patient and lifting her to check her ears with the auriscope and spoon the Panadol into the little mouth. Gemma watched her swallow and gently lowered her to the bed again.

'There's a chap on the veranda who said he'd wait because the garage couldn't fix your car without the key, and he'll do it when he drops you back,' Ros said as she came back in with a bowl of water and began sponging Maggie's feverish body, while the child relaxed back into a healing sleep.

Gemma nodded but her mind was still on her patient. 'How long was she unconscious?' she asked as she wrote up her notes.

Michael and Suzi looked at each other, then Suzi explained. 'She suddenly cried out and dropped to the floor, no tremors or rigour like the ordinary epileptic kids. She's had little drop attacks on other visits, but usually tells us she feels sick, and heads straight for her bed. Sometimes the feeling goes away, and sometimes she half passes out, but this time she seemed deeply unconscious. We lifted her on to the bed, but there were no signs of it passing.'

'Suzi went straight for the Valium and water we had ready in the fridge,' Michael continued, hugging his wife again. 'It might have been five minutes since she dropped, by the time she'd mixed it and administered it, and another minute before we saw any response.'

'Let's check her history, then ring her parents and explain what's happened and see what they want us to do. They'll know if she's likely to have another one, or if she should be hospitalised. If you're willing to keep her here and they agree, I can see no reason why she shouldn't stay.'

They left Ros with Maggie and walked through to the kitchen, which was the hub of the household.

'Have you tied up the other four?' Gemma asked, as the quiet in the usually rowdy house seemed unbelievable.

Michael laughed. 'Suzi's gone to check on them now and phone Maggie's family,' he explained. 'But they did get a fright when Maggie passed out on us. They finished their tea in silence then disappeared like lambs to the television-room and have hardly been heard from since.'

'I'd have to see it to believe it,' Gemma remarked drily. 'Three of those kids are usually swinging from the rafters at this time of night. I've been here before, remember!'

'We've got an extra helper.' Michael smiled as he explained. 'He's a university student and I think he pays his way through uni with magic tricks. He's got those boys right under his thumb, with promises of tricks as rewards for good behaviour!'

'What a genius!' Gemma agreed, knowing how hard it was to bribe these children whose diets were too strictly controlled to allow sweets as rewards.

'Here's Maggie's file.' Michael handed her the plastic-covered book. 'I'll call your chauffeur in for some coffee.'

Gemma was startled. She'd forgotten about the man, and had taken little notice of Ros's remark. She concentrated on the file, noticing that these small attacks were usually triggered by infection and rarely recurred if the infection was treated. Antibiotics were usually introduced immediately and Panadol repeated four-hourly. She checked the allergy list in the file, then turned over to the 'Usual Drugs Given' notations.

'Her mum says she should be fine,' Suzi announced proudly as she returned, nodding at the stranger whom Michael was ushering into the kitchen. 'She's never had a recurrence of a bad seizure within a few months, but they do keep her temperature down with Panadol——'

'And I'll leave some Amoxil syrup for her as well,' Gemma interrupted as Suzi repeated the written instructions. 'Can you manage her through the night?'

'We can tonight,' Suzi responded wryly, turning to acknowledge the man whom Michael had introduced as Simon Griffiths. 'Last night we had no extra staff and Gemma was here till the wee hours of the morning, keeping watch over an outbreak of chickenpox. Tonight, all the other kids' temperatures are down and we have two extra staff.'

'It's always the way,' Michael added. 'Now for coffee! We know Gemma's hot, sweet tastes but how do you have it?'

Thrusting the file into Suzi's hands, Gemma said quickly, 'We can't stay. This man—er—Simon——' she ignored the quizzical glance the stranger was casting her way '—was at the surgery when I left and kindly drove me out here. He has to get home to his friend.'

'I'm in no hurry,' was the infuriating reply, and

Gemma stifled an impulse to stamp her foot yet again. He'd come bursting into her life, hurled accusations at her, and was now behaving, in front of her friends, as if he were the original Mr Nice-Guy.

'Well, I am,' she snapped, then felt all eyes turn towards her. 'I've got a date,' she added lamely, not knowing why she felt obliged to lie.

'Well, in that case, the coffee must certainly be cancelled,' Simon Griffiths responded gallantly, and bowed her towards the door. 'At your service, madam,' he said, and nodded a smiling farewell to Michael and Suzi.

'The Amoxil is on the kitchen bench with instructions. You've got plenty of Panadol Elixir?'

'Yes, we'll manage,' Suzi assured her, hurrying her towards the door as if she sensed Gemma's reluctance to leave the familiar environment and the safety of her friends' company.

Simon and Michael stood chatting easily on the veranda, and turned as she emerged. 'So you see, this service couldn't exist here without our trusty local GP,' Michael was saying with obvious sincerity, and Gemma felt colour stealing into her cheeks.

'Mind your flattery,' she warned, crossing the veranda and stepping out of the light to hide her embarrassment. She sensed the man's presence before he took her arm in a carefully impersonal grasp and led her across the uneven yard.

An uneasy silence hovered in the air as they fastened seatbelts and Simon fired the engine, then swung the big four-wheel drive back on to the road.

'Status epilepticus?' he queried softly.

She spun around to face him, but his eyes were fixed on the road ahead. Long, lean fingers held the wheel, and Gemma watched their movement as she reined in her racing mind.

'What do you know about status epilepticus?' she asked supiciously.

'Very little these days,' he admitted with a certain ruefulness. 'The name popped into my brain while Michael was telling me about the little girl. It's used to define seizure activity that's likely to last longer than thirty minutes, isn't it? Prolonged unconsciousness that requires medical intervention before the patient regains consciousness?'

Nodding slowly, Gemma explained, 'It's always a worry with Maggie. Although, because her seizures aren't typical, there's less risk of mortality, she can, and does, lose consciousness for long periods of time. If it's prolonged, that causes further brain damage, which exacerbates the condition. It's one of those vicious cirle things!'

'Drop attacks rather than tonic clonic seizures?' he asked with interest, but the second show of medical knowledge finally penetrated Gemma's brain, banishing all thoughts of Maggie and the classification of epileptic seizures.

'You're a doctor?' She couldn't believe it and knew her tone betrayed her incredulity.

'Why not?'

'Well. . .' she started but could not continue. Grasping at her wayward thoughts, she blurted out the first thing that came into her head. 'If you're a doctor, why did your friend come to me?'

The question seemed to trigger others, and, without waiting for a response, she hurried on, 'And surely you should have seen that the woman needed professional help? And understood that a doctor's appointment about childhood sniffles with two wild juveniles erupting round the place wasn't going to be the answer! And you accuse *me* of unprofessional conduct!' Her voice rose steadily as her indignation increased.

They were back in the town and the street-lights lit up his face, enabling her to see the thin set of his lips. He was either angered by her attack, or. . .she studied him suspiciously. . .trying not to laugh? The thought fuelled her rage.

'Are you always this fiery or is it just lack of sleep?' The teasing hint of humour was unmistakable. He was laughing at her!

'It's none of your business what I am,' she yelled at him, clenching her fists in her lap as she fought an urge to batter them against his rock-like frame.

'I'm only asking,' he replied smoothly, his lips twitching as if he was having difficulty controlling a smile. 'Now——' he pulled up behind her car '—how about you open the boot then take my car back to your place to get ready for your date while I change that tyre?'

'You don't have to change the tyre,' she muttered, suspicion and anger warring within her. 'I am quite capable of doing it.' She crossed her fingers as she spoke, knowing that the closest she had ever come to such a task was watching her father do it many years earlier.

'And keep your boyfriend waiting while you get ready? Do you realise it's after nine? He must be a patient chap!' He had turned in his seat to speak to her, unsnapping his seatbelt as he spoke, his fingers invasively close to hers as she prepared to get out of his car.

'I'm not going out,' she mumbled frustratedly, wondering how she was going to shake off this persistent Sir Galahad. 'I've got all night to do it!'

'You told a lie?' His incredulous tone made it sound like a major crime wave and, for the second time that afternoon, she felt her temper simmering dangerously.

'I didn't want to be hanging around out there,

disrupting the carers, and taking their time and attention away from the kids,' she defended herself. And I didn't want a cosy cup of coffee and social chat with you, she thought but did not say. Shifting slightly in her seat, Gemma reached out to open the door in a bid to escape his invasive presence.

'If you'll agree to have a quick bite to eat with me then it wouldn't have been a lie.'

'Have dinner with you?' Incredulity pitched her voice into shrieking range!

'I know you're tired but we've both got to eat,' he explained smoothly. 'If you want to freshen up first, I'll drop you at your home, and then collect you when the tyre's fixed. We'll grab a meal and you can drive your own car home after it.'

It sounded eminently practical and matter-of-fact and Gemma could only shake her head in bemusement.

'You can't want to have dinner with a complete stranger,' she argued defiantly. 'Unless you want to continue criticising me for unprofessional conduct. And what about your friend? Have the twins become too much for you to take? Do you need some time out? Don't you care that she needs your support?'

'Whoa there, lady!' he cried, throwing up his arms in a mocking gesture of surrender. 'My "friend", as you call her, has taken the boys out visiting, and I would like to take you to dinner to apologise for my earlier behaviour.'

'You don't have to do that,' Gemma told him, confused by her own wildly swinging reactions to this man.

'Indeed I do. I should have realised that Anne's version of the events was likely to be highly coloured, and I do see now that she needs professional help. Can't we go out as medical colleagues and discuss it in a civilised manner? I'd also like to know a lot more about the set-up at Orana. How it's funded and who runs it; how it was started. I didn't realise such places existed.'

The invitation tempted her. The drive in the cooler night air had banished the dragging weariness she'd been feeling as she'd left the surgery. It was months since she'd spoken to another doctor, apart from hurried consultations over the phone with specialists in Craigstown, the nearest city. The isolation she felt from others in her profession was one of the few drawbacks in working out here at Grange Bay.

He waited in silence, as if allowing her all the time in the world to think over his proposal, but when she nodded he smiled broadly and she saw the gleam of strong white teeth flash in the dimness of the car.

'Where do you live?' he asked, quickly turning on the engine again and pulling out from the kerb as if he was afraid she'd change her mind.

'Straight on up the hill,' she told him. 'It's the last house on the left. I could walk to and from work but, as I usually do house-calls at lunchtime and after work, I need to have the car.' She realised she was chattering to hide a peculiar unease.

He continued on up the hill and turned into her drive. She slipped the keys of her car on to the dashboard for him, and opened the door to jump out. 'I'll have a quick shower and walk back down the hill to meet you,' she told him, dragging her bag out behind her.

'You could leave that in this car and I'll transfer it to your car when I get down there,' he offered.

'Oh, yeah?' she murmured with a provocative grin, her mood lightening at the thought of the evening ahead. 'Now that would be unprofessional conduct!'

She shut the car door carefully and walked up the winding path, throught the mini-rainforest, to the veranda of her home. Sensors picked up her movement and flooded the entry with light, and she heard the big car turn and glide quietly back down the hill.

She looked out over the lights of the town to the inky blackness of the sea, her keen eyes seeking out the flickering lights of the fishing fleet.

They'll have a good night, she thought automatically as she felt the faint north-easterly breeze linger against her cheek. Having bestowed her silent blessing on the boats, she turned away towards the door, and, with an unfamiliar acceleration in her heartbeats, hurried into the house to shower and change. She had a date!

CHAPTER TWO

SHOWERING was easy, and deciding what to wear was not difficult. It might be midsummer, and the night air balmy, but all three of the restaurants in town were air-conditioned, and could be fiercely cold. She pulled on silk trousers in a deep taupe colour, and matched them with a cream silk top that had a low rounded neckline, slightly padded shoulders and short sleeves. She'd take her new, light, patterned anorak to slip around her shoulders. Its vibrant tones of orange, gold and brown made it the perfect choice, flattering her colouring and deepening the honey-brown of her eyes.

Make-up wasn't much of a problem either. Her skin was lightly tanned all the time, although she protected it every day with lashings of UV cream. A touch of colour on her high, slanting cheekbones to take away the tired paleness, a slick of dark liner across her eyelids to detract attention from the dark shadows beneath her eyes, mascara on her long, dark lashes, and a subtle, coral-toned lipstick, smoothed across lips that were too full for beauty.

She stared critically at the result, wondering if she needed a film of powder, then deciding against it. Gemma sighed. The face was OK, but the hair! The mouth in the mirror twisted in a wry grimace as she looked at the long plait that hung limply down her back, damp where the shower-cap had failed to protect it.

'Get it cut,' her mother kept telling her; 'it would suit you really short, or even shoulder-length, but you can't do anything with hair that long.'

Sighing heavily, she removed the elastic band that held it in place and then ran her fingers through the twisting strands, teasing it out into a kinky mass. She picked up her brush and began the long, slow strokes that would restore it to order, and bring back the shine. She couldn't cut it yet! Not while her warmest and closest memories of her father were of the times when he would sit and brush her hair!

With the ease of long practice she smoothed it to a fall of honey-brown silk, softer and more lustrous than the clothes she had put on, then with deft fingers she lifted a heavy swath from each side of her face and drew them up high on the back of her head, where she fixed them with a tortoiseshell clasp, in such a way that the lighter, sun-bleached strands now lay across the top of the waving, silken mass.

'It's all I can do,' she muttered defiantly at her image, answering her mother's gentle chiding although she was a thousand miles away.

'I've brought your car up and run it into the carport.'

The voice startled her and she turned from the mirror with a final searching glance.

Again a sense of invasion hit Gemma. Her little house had always been her haven—a secure retreat from the world. Perched on poles that had been sunk deep into the sloping hillside, it was protected by the bush behind, and her sheltering, palm-filled garden. Polished wooden floors were decorated with a scattering of rugs, but her footsteps echoed hollowly tonight as she walked through the open living area and, for the first time, the house seemed empty! Almost lonely!

Ignoring these presentiments, she came swiftly out on to the veranda, pulling the front door closed behind her, before crossing to where Simon Griffiths stood, looking out over the lightening sea.

'Are they fishing boats out there?' he asked, hearing her approach but not turning from his first compelling glimpse of the rising moon.

'Yes, they're our boats,' she told him, coming to share the magic of nature's show.

It was almost full, the rising moon, huge and slightly misshapen, an orangy yellow orb coming slowly into full view as if pushed on to a stage by unseen hands. Rising cumbersomely above the horizon, it lit a broadening path across the restless waters, spreading a band of sparkling silver light like a tempting pathway towards the shore.

'Beautiful, isn't it?' she murmured, obscurely glad to be sharing this moment with someone.

'It is!' he agreed, then turned to look down into her face, which was still filled with the wonder of it. 'Very beautiful.'

He lifted his hand and with one finger touched her cheek, and it seemed that his eyes, still too shadowed for her to judge a colour, sent a special message into her heart.

Gemma turned away, her breath catching in her throat. The hectic Christmas holiday period was no time for her treacherous heart to be looking for company—especially not the type a transient tourist could offer!

'Shall we go?' she suggested, wanting him off her veranda before his presence left a shadow she would see for days.

'My carriage awaits you,' he replied, bowing again in his mock-chivalrous manner.

Gemma grinned and led the way, stepping daintily ahead of him through the dense jungle path. There was a sense of fun in this stranger that warmed her troubled spirit and made her set aside the sharp pang of regret she'd experienced only seconds earlier.

'You've brought both cars up,' she called back over her shoulder as she recognised the silhouette of his Range Rover at the kerb. 'That was quick work.'

'Good exercise,' he responded. 'It made me realise how unfit I've become, when I puffed and panted lifting your spare out of the boot.'

'Thank you for fixing it,' she said warmly, turning towards him with genuine friendliness for the first time since they had met. 'I do appreciate it.'

'Just don't forget to drop the flat one into the garage in the morning. You can't afford to be without a spare. Perhaps I should leave my car with you tonight, in case you're called out again.'

He sounded so concerned for her well-being that she felt a glowing warmth through her body, and a sudden longing to have someone to share the petty day-to-day problems that seemed to beset her.

'I should be all right,' she told him, smiling up into his anxious face. 'It's after ten now, and by the time we've eaten it will be close to midnight.'

'Do you turn pumpkins into carriages at midnight?' His eyes twinkled down at her, and she smiled again.

'No, but the local rotary club decided it wasn't safe for me to be out and about at all hours of the night on my own. They worked out a rostered call system that provides me with a driver. We work it through the pager. I activate mine, and whoever has the rotary pager at home with them comes in response.'

'There's obviously more to a country practice than one sees on TV,' he remarked, taking her arm to help her up into the car before walking around the bonnet and climbing in beside her.

'Where to? You're the local.'

'There's not much choice at this time of night,' she said with a laugh. 'The Fish Kettle would be the only place still open, I think. You turn right into the main street and follow that to the esplanade, then right again. You can't miss it. They have steak and some pasta dishes if you don't like seafood.'

'Do grown-up people come to seaside resorts if they don't like seafood?' he mocked roguishly, his eyes on the road as they came into the main street, where families still strolled and teenagers clumped on street corners.

'Grown-up people usually come to bring their children,' she responded smartly, and, unable to resist the impulse, added, 'Or their friend's children!'

'She worries you? My friend?' He spun the big car to the right, and pulled up under one of the shaggy casuarinas that lined the beachfront.

Gemma sighed. In more ways than one, she would have liked to say, but she stuck to medical matters. After all, it was as colleagues that they were dining, however much his sudden appearance in her life had reawakened her hidden longing to have a special 'friend'.

'I should have done more for her this morning,' she admitted, 'but as the boys had knocked over Willie, and were proceeding to dismantle him into his two hundred and six separate pieces, it wasn't the right moment for deep and meaningful discussion.'

'You keep a skeleton in your surgery?'

'Only in the darkest corner of it,' she joked. 'I find it amuses some people, and it certainly helps break the ice with awkward adolescents.'

She opened the door and jumped down from her perch, before he had time to walk around the car and hold out a helping hand. Simon Griffiths was arousing too many odd emotions with his presence without having him continually firing her nerve-endings with his light, impersonal touch.

'Nice to see you out and about, Gemma,' Grant

Louden greeted her, nodding at her escort as he ushered them into the cool, discreetly lit interior.

Gemma introduced the two men, adding, 'Simon's a doctor, here with some friends for the holidays. He came to my rescue when my car had a flat tyre,' she went on to explain as if driven to excuse herself for being out with a strange man this late at night!

She saw the speculative glint in Grant's eyes and then caught the teasing gleam of humour in Simon's as he acknowledged her embarrassement.

'May we sit on the deck?' she asked quickly, to defuse the tension that only she could feel.

'You may indeed,' Grant affirmed, and led the way through the potted plants that provided privacy between the tables at his popular restaurant.

He reached the table set in a corner of the deck, looking out through the fringing trees at the top of the dunes to the moonlit sea beyond, and dropped two menus on it.

'I've some Tasmanian scallops, grilled as kebas, and the fish of the day is fresh tuna, lightly seared over hot coals and served with baked capsicum and eggplant, and a trickle of balsamic vinegar. Would you like a drink while you think about food?'

Gemma looked towards her companion, realising that she knew nothing about the man. He raised one eyebrow with a quirky grin, and knew immediately that he had read her thought, or, even worse, had shared it.

'Will you share a bottle of white wine with me?'

She nodded, glad that she didn't have to speak as she fought another irrational tug of attraction.

'I've a lovely Leconfield Coonawarra Rhine Riesling on ice, if you want something light, or a Basedow's Chardonnay Semillon?' Grant offered.

'Is that the Black Label?' Simon asked, and received

an answering smile and nod from the restaurateur. The talk moved on to the complexities of wine and Gemma sank back into her chair and opened the menu.

Had Simon seen how proud Grant was of his knowledge of food and wine? Gemma wondered. This might be a little backwater only recently discovered by the city folk who flocked to the seaside each summer, but Grant was determined to maintain a level of excellence equal to any in the cities.

'We'll have the Basedow's,' Simon was saying, 'and I'll have the tuna. It sounds delicious and it's far too late to be thinking for oneself!'

'Gemma?' Grant's hand rested on her shoulder for a moment, a touch so light she might have imagined it!

'Scallops for me, if you serve them with your spiced rice, and perhaps a salad, thanks, Grant.'

He moved off, and, for a moment, Simon watched him walk away, his expressive eyes full of questions. Then he turned back towards her and smiled. Light flared behind him from a sweet citronella-scented flame in a bamboo holder, and, for the first time, she realised what an incredibly attractive man he was. The bits and pieces of him that she had studied surreptitiously added up to a whole that had a devastating charm, especially when he smiled!

No wonder her body was behaving erratically. This was a man with the kind of magnetism one saw in film stars or read about in books, and yet there was nothing particularly special—nothing you could pin down as perfect or handsome!

'You look like Alice in Wonderland landing at the bottom of the rabbit hole,' he said softly, his gaze roving over her face with an almost physical caress.

'I've always pictured Alice as a blue-eyed blonde,' Gemma retorted.

'Whereas you're a woodland sylph, all honey-gold

and brown!' His smile deepened and his eyes held hers enmeshed. 'It was more your expression that brought Alice to mind.'

'Terrified?' She smiled gaily, hoping to hide her inner confusion.

'No,' he answered seriously, 'more surprised, and slightly apprehensive, yet determined to face whatever has to be faced.'

'Don't tell me,' she retorted facetiously, hoping to fend off his challenging perceptions. 'You're a psychiatrist, and you've practised pretty little speeches like that to put your patients at ease when they first sit on your couch.'

'I specialised in orthopaedics, actually,' he told her, but the mood was broken and she was both relieved and saddened.

'Where do you practise?' It was the obvious question and would lead into nice, safe, medical conversation, which was what she wanted. Wasn't it?

'Melbourne,' he replied, naming the one east-coast city that was not within reasonable travelling distance of Grange Bay.

'Then you're far from the usual summer haunts of Victorians. We have Sydney and Brisbane visitors "discovering" our little haven, but it's a long way from your home.'

'It was an influx of Victorians that put Noosa Heads on the map,' he replied, mentioning the Queensland village that had developed into a cosmopolitan resort through southern tourists and southern investment.

Gemma nodded, but said seriously, 'I wouldn't like Grange Bay to become another Noosa.'

'Youngsters like you shouldn't dread change,' he commented, his lips drawing back in a slight smile, and his eyes glittering with his amusement.

'I grew up in Grange Bay,' she confessed, 'and, while

I know we need the tourists, and accept how much good they do the town, I would hate to see the essential spirit of the place altered beyond recognition.'

'Isn't it the people in the place who make the spirit what it is?' he challenged, and she sensed a depth behind the light bantering manner.

'But people can change,' she said sadly. 'They see a chance to make some quick money, sell property for amounts they had never dreamed of, then don't seem to know what to do. They become displaced.'

Grant approached with a long green bottle and proffered it tenderly towards Simon, who nodded, then watched as Grant removed the cork and poured a little into a glass.

The ritual continued as Simon lifted the glass to his lips and sipped at the pale liquid. Gemma's eyes followed every movement, seeing his hand reach out to grasp the stem of the glass, his lips part to take in the wine. She held her breath, and wet her own dry lips with the tip of her tongue, then the ceremony ended as Simon accepted Grant's choice.

'Lovely,' he affirmed, setting the glass back down on the table with a satisfied smirk, while Gemma collected her straying thoughts and wondered what she'd been talking about.

'Do the people who sell out stay in town?' Simon was asking as Grant moved away.

'They usually dash off on a trip around the world first,' she replied, recognising where the conversation had been and returning to it with a singular gladness. 'Then they come back and find out how expensive it will be to buy back into something in town, and that seems to be when the trouble starts!'

'It happens everywhere, Gemma,' he observed, and she started at his use of her name. Looking up, she saw him smiling at her across the table as he raised his glass in salute.

Again she felt the potency of his attraction, and reached for her frosted glass, raised it in response, then drank a quick gulp of the cold, clear wine to hide the turmoil he was causing within her body.

'What did Suzi use on the little epileptic girl?'

The question startled her, but she welcomed the return to the neutrality of a medical topic.

'Her family uses Valium, 10mg administered rectally for quick absorption. The carers at Orana knew to do the same. It's a ridiculous system, because the drug is only available by prescription as a tablet here, which means they must keep sterile water in the refrigerator, then heat it and attempt to dissolve an almost insoluble tablet in the water, before administering it with a syringe.'

'An intravenous injection would surely be a better way to go,' Simon agreed, 'but, if I remember rightly, it has to be administered very slowly——'

'And it's often impossible for a parent or care-giver to find a vein in a little child! There's too much risk!' Gemma interrupted to explain.

'Not easy for trained medicos either at times,' he added wryly, and Gemma found herself smiling back.

'We've had kids at Orana who came originally from New Zealand, and they have a wonderful liquid Valium available in disposable plastic dispensers. All a parent has to do is snip the top, insert the tube and squeeze, but do you think we can convince the authorities to pass it for Australian use?'

He murmured sympathetically, but something in his tone caught her attention, and she looked up to see amusement creasing the skin around his eyes, and dimpling his cheeks, although his lips remained firmly closed.

'I do tend to get carried away,' Gemma admitted with a rueful grin, 'but I rarely have anyone I can complain to, who actually understands what I'm saying—except for the local chemist. He's a dear old chap, but he's known me since I was born and shows an alarming tendency to run and hide in his dispensary whenever I walk into his shop.'

She looked disarmingly into his eyes and saw the smile break across his face again, and heard the deep rumble of delighted laughter.

'I shall consider it a public duty to take you out to dinner each evening and listen to your complaints,' he assured her, and she felt a fiery heat spread upwards through her body, and stain her cheeks with colour.

Knowing no words to deflect his joking invitation, she ignored it, looking up to welcome Grant back to their table with a quick, flashing smile.

The food was beautifully presented, looking more like delicate artistic arrangements than edible delights, and the spicy fragrance trickled upwards, sparking Gemma's appetite.

'It smells delicious,' she told Grant, picking up her fork and scooping up a mouthful of rice, 'and tastes even better.'

He grinned at her then turned to watch Simon's reaction to the colourful array of flavours on his plate, leaving them alone only when he was satisfied that both meals had met with his diners' approval.

'Is he the chef as well as the owner?' Simon asked as Grant left.

'Yes, although he has an apprentice and a number of kitchen staff. He's a local who went away to do his training but came back. Each year, he closes the restaurant for two months after the Christmas season and travels overseas to keep up with what's happening in the culinary world.'

'And how do you keep up with what's happening in the medical world? Can you close up for a few months each year?'

'Hardly!' Gemma replied, pausing in her enjoyment of the food to have another sip of her wine. 'I'm lucky if I can get a locum for a fortnight, and, although I try to make it at a time when I can attend a conference or series of seminars, it doesn't always work out that way.'

'It's not much of a holiday for you either!' He sounded disapproving, but whether at her lack of continuing education or her disrupted holidays she couldn't tell.

'I keep up with the latest research and developments through all the magazines that are available, and have regular trips across to Craigstown when they have guest speakers or AMA meetings over there. We're not totally isolated out here.' She was aware that she sounded defensive, but, although her professional isolation worried her, she knew there was little she could do about it.

When he did not reply, she looked up at him and realised that he was watching her with an intentness that heightened her concern, and compelled her to continue speaking.

'The fact of the matter is, this practice isn't big enough to support two doctors, although one and a half would be great.'

'Is there no neighbouring town which could support another half?' He sounded genuinely interested in the problem, and she felt again the subtle allure of having someone with whom she could share her thoughts and theories.

'Unfortunately not. The nearest town is forty kilometres back on the highway, and it has a twice-a-week doctor from Craigstown. I do more work there than he does, as many of the people in the area will come here rather than go to town, or wait for his visits.'

She bent her head over the plate, forking up the last mouthful of rice. Frustration was building up inside her, as it inevitably did when she considered her workload. It was better to keep going and not think about it, but this man had dredged her problem back up to the surface of her mind.

Putting down her fork and pushing the plate from her with a small murmur of satisfaction, she looked up to see his light eyes regarding her intently, the tiny lines at the corner of them creased enough to signify a faint amusement.

'If I'd had a particle of sense,' she told him firmly, 'I'd have married a fellow student when I finished university. One man with a wife working part-time would have been ideal!'

Simon's faint amusement turned to laughter, startling Gemma, who had merely said out loud what she had been thinking for the past two years.

'I'm sure there'd have been no shortage of offers if you'd asked around,' he teased, a broad smile deepening the creases in his cheeks to hidden dimples.

'It must be a long time since you went through if you think that!' she said crossly, torn between annoyance at his laughter and suspicion that he might be flirting with her. 'All the boys I knew had their sights set on specialities. The days when the height of ambition was to be a small-town GP are long gone—if they ever did exist!'

'The boyfriend refused to come to heel, huh? What speciality did he choose?'

Again he startled her with his perception. Had he heard a faint echo of old bitterness in her voice? She thought of Alex so seldom these days, she could not believe this stranger could have divined his place in her student life.

'Eyes,' she said briefly, slamming the door tightly shut on memories she did not want intruding. 'But that was a long time ago, and, if you think I'm pining for a lost love, you're wrong!'

'Of course,' he agreed smoothly. 'Your only regret must be that you wasted time on him when you could have been looking for someone who was better GP material.'

His eyes shone with a teasing humour, although his mobile face was a blandly serious mask.

'Well, it would have been more sensible!' she declared stoutly, then grinned at him as she accepted how ridiculous her regrets must seem to this stranger.

'They didn't realise what they were missing,' he responded with a quirky grin.

Her eyes were caught, and held, by his, and again she felt a flickering of fire along her nerve-endings and a surging warmth in her blood.

'Time you were in bed, Gemma!'

Grant's voice behind her broke the spell.

'Want to close shop, do you?' Simon asked lazily.

'Partly that, and partly the fact that this kid is up at dawn to torture some of us poor citizens with what she calls her health regime.' Grant moved close to the back of her chair and rested both his hands on her shoulders as he answered Simon. It was a protective gesture, she knew, but would it also look possessive? And why should she care?

Simon cocked one eyebrow enquiringly, and embarrassed by Grant's words and behaviour, Gemma rushed into speech again.

'I've two patients who've had mild heart attacks and another five, including Grant here, with cholesterol levels high enough to be in grave danger of heart disease, so I've lumped them all together—'

'And, instead of letting us sleep peacefully in our little beds, she has us up at six every morning, walking the beach while she prises out the secret sins we've committed against her precious diet.'

'Hard on a chef,' Simon agreed sympathetically.

'Hard be blowed,' Gemma argued. 'All he's had to do is learn to eat more carbohydrates, and use them on his menus. Now people know they can eat here without risking their lives!'

'And has it worked?'

Again Simon showed the interest that she found immensely seductive.

'After three weeks of excercise combined with a diet that is made up of seventy-five per cent complex carbohydrates and where the fat provides less than ten per cent of total calories, I've got them all down at least twenty per cent. Grant's serum cholesterol has come down from 8.8 to 5.6mmol per litre, which is great, but not sufficiently low to have him slacken off,' she finished warningly.

'On the beach at six?' Simon asked in a faint voice, as if the thought of such early activity was frightening.

'On the dot,' Gemma confirmed. 'We've all got other things to fit into the day, and Grant, at least, can go back to bed when we've finished, unlike some of us.' She shrugged his hands off her shoulders, and pushed her chair back from the table.

'Well, that being the case, I should get you home,' Simon suggested.

'Can we have the bill, Grant?' Gemma asked, her voice cool as she hid a contrary flicker of annoyance with him for forcing the evening to an abrupt conclusion, although the practical part of her mind conceded that it was time for bed.

'I'll fix it up,' Simon was saying, but her disappointment, and the sense of loss that accompanied it, made her feel distinctly annoyed.

'There's no need for that,' she told him sharply. 'I'd prefer to pay my share. That's what colleagues do, after all.'

He bowed his head, accepting her decree, as Grant returned and placed the bill discreetly on the table. She snatched it up but felt Simon's eyes on her again, and sensed his ever-present amusement. She studied the slip of paper, nibbling at her bottom lip as she divided the total.

'Can we afford it?' he asked lightly. 'Shall I have to sell the house? Tell me the worst!'

'It's twenty-five dollars each, if we leave a small tip, which we don't have to do, but it makes the mathematics easier,' she said hurriedly, embarrassed now that they were discussing money.

'That's fine,' he replied, but continued to watch her closely.

Flustered by his steady regard, she reached down towards the floor, feeling for her handbag, then pushed back her chair and looked under the table.

'Lost something?' he asked evenly, his lips twitching again in that light, teasing fashion.

'My handbag——' she started, then remembered. She'd heard his voice, come out on to the veranda and stood to watch the moon. Then they'd left. She'd pulled the door shut and they'd walked away! She didn't have her handbag, or any money to pay the share she had insisted on paying!

'What if I pay tonight, and you pay next time?' he suggested, chuckling at her discomfort. She was about to nod when something stopped her. Much as she had enjoyed herself, she was uncertain about a next time. The sophisticated dalliance this stranger seemed to be offering was too far beyond her limited experience to be considered with anything other than alarm.

'I can slip inside and get you the money when you drop me home,' she said quickly.

'I might not want to wait!' He was folding notes inside the bill folder and closing it as he spoke, so she could not see his eyes or read his face. Yet, somehow, Gemma sensed a hidden meaning behind the lightly spoken words, and she shivered.

He looked up and caught her eyes again, and it seemed as if time stood still. The mild breeze tickled her neck, playing delicately in her hair. It carried with it the tantalisingly sweet smell of the pandanus palm, and imprinted its impression on her heightened senses. The soothing sea sounds murmured in her ears, and the taste of the wine lingered on her lips. It was an instant that could never be repeated; a moment like any other, yet taking on a significance that she could not understand.

'Sit on that independence of yours, Gemma, and let the man pay.'

She hadn't heard Grant return, but his voice brought back the present, and she nodded her head, acknowledging something that wasn't quite defeat.

They left soon after, and drove back up the hill to her home with only some murmured comments about the meal. The tiredness that had been held at bay since meeting Simon now swamped back over her like a heavy weight.

'It was a lovely evening,' she told him as she picked up her bunch of keys and slipped out of the car. She held the door open and looked back up at him, darkly still behind the wheel. 'Thank you for coming to my rescue, and for the meal.'

There was much, much more she wanted to say—Let me repay it some time, might sound casual enough, or, How long are you staying? Maybe we'll meet again—but it would sound as if she was encouraging him, and that was the last thing she wanted to do. A holiday romance with a visiting fellow professional would be hard to live down—and maybe even harder to get over! And, of course, there was his friend!

'Thanks again,' she murmured and she turned away into the sanctuary of her garden and the safety of her home.

CHAPTER THREE

GEMMA woke at five-thirty, her body clock functioning automatically in spite of a restless night. Sheer exhaustion had, eventually, brought the release of sleep, but not before Gemma had tossed and turned, her mind disturbed by the betrayal of her body, and the unmistakable way it had responded to Simon Griffiths.

The morning air was cool and refreshing as she pulled on a pair of old shorts and a baggy cotton T-shirt, and caught her hair back into a ponytail with a brightly coloured band. Sticking to her own routine gave her control over her life, she decided—a life she had chosen, and one she loved.

She drove down to the beachfront to meet her band of walkers, feeling the familiar surging delight as her eyes took in the silvery beauty of the new day, already warmed by the sun, but not yet coloured. Night tides had swept the beach clean of all signs of the previous day's invasion of sun-worshippers, and it lay like a curving golden carpet, between the edging rocks and the water. The sea was calm, a muted pearly grey, white-flecked along the shore where small waves broke with a quiet rhythm.

Her little group clustered at the top of the steps that led down to the beach, stretching, shaking their legs and arms, and, as usual, she knew, protesting about the earliness of the hour and her determination to get them fit.

'Morning, Gemma!'

'Lovely day.'

'Nice weather for the tourists!'

The greetings rarely altered; it was part of what she loved about Grange Bay, this predictability. She smiled and waved a cheery good morning, her eyes quickly checking that they were all present.

He was standing with Grant at the back of the group, but, even from a distance, she could see the mocking glint in his eyes, and her mind whirled back into the confusion of the night before.

She turned away and led off down the steps, walking briskly and talking determinedly to Mary Parsons who, with her husband, Dave, ran the only bakery in town and had been known to over-indulge in her own tempting delights. A mild heart attack had frightened Mary sufficiently for her to accept Gemma's health regime, and stick to it religiously.

Talking was no help! Mary thrived on gossip!

'Who's the new guy?' was her first question, when Gemma paused for breath.

'He's a visitor from Melbourne,' Gemma told her. 'He came to my rescue last night.' She regaled Mary with a brief summary of the evening's events as casually as possible, before adding, 'He and Grant hit it off, talking wine and food. Maybe that's why he decided to join the walk this morning.'

'Maybe!' was the non-committal response, but something in Mary's tone made Gemma look suspiciously at her, then quicken the pace towards the low headland that sheltered the beach from southerly winds.

A pair of long-billed oyster-catchers pierced the sand in search of breakfast, barely bothering to move out of the way of the little gaggle of humans, who walked briskly past them each morning. Up the grassy slope Gemma led, and down into the little cove below, a deep shallow inlet, with rocky sides, much beloved by the amateur fisherman, who flocked to the town in the summer holidays.

The sea was calm today, but the rocky point could be treacherous, and Gemma always checked automatically, counting the number of motionless figures concentrating determinedly on their sport.

From the southern end of the cove, their way led back along a track through the coastal scrub, following the top of a sandy, brush-covered ridge that brought them down into the town. The idle chatter usually stopped as they climbed the ridge, and—usually—Gemma appreciated the silence.

Each morning, she would breathe deeply as she took in the glory of the views to north and south, and the matchless sweep of ocean, now deeply blue far out, and shading back to translucent aquamarine where the low swell broke against the shore. It was a time for confirming her decision to return to Grange Bay—a time when she felt the beauty of the place renew her love for it and confirm that here was where she belonged.

'Unbelievable view!'

Unmistakably Simon!

He must have passed the others on the climb and fallen in behind her on the narrow bush track.

'I think so,' she said simply, quickening her steps as if to flee his intrusive presence.

'I thought I might take the twins to the beach this morning, if you could see Anne on her own for a few minutes? It might come better from you than from me, this business of seeing a psychologist.'

That was all he wanted! Gemma felt the breath leave her body in a great rush, although she hadn't known she'd been holding it. But the relief was overlaid with a feeling of chagrin, and she twitched her shoulders irritably as if trying to shake off the alien mood.

'I'll tell my receptionist to make a time for her if she rings, but there's no one here in Grange Bay who could help her. Surely you'd know of a good psychologist or family counsellor in Melbourne?'

'What about Craigstown?' he asked, ignoring her damping comments. 'There must be someone you could recommend there.' His voice came persistently over her shoulder, irritating Gemma with the concern that she herself had awoken.

'It depends how long you're here for,' she answered shortly. 'There's not much point starting with one counsellor if she can't continue seeing him or her. And most of the psychologists in town will be heavily booked leading up to Christmas and probably on holidays afterwards.'

'You're saying people can't have troubles over the holidays? It's too inconvenient for the local specialists?' The aggression that had been absent from his voice since the first few minutes of their meeting on the steps was back, but she sensed he was testing her, pushing her for some reason of his own.

Your patients have to wait on your return from holidays, she wanted to say, but was that what he was trying to goad her into saying? Most orthopaedic operations were elective, she knew, and could be planned to suit both patient and doctor. Maybe her unspoken criticism was unfair! She collected her thoughts, oblivious to the strengthening heat of the sunshine on her back and the rustle of the small animals and birds in the bush around them.

'I've said I'll see her,' she repeated, returning to the safer subject of his 'friend', 'and I will do what I can to help. I'm well aware that special celebrations like Christmas tend to exacerbate personal problems rather than solve them. But I can't promise anything, especially as she seems to have resented me at our first meeting.'

'I can explain that to her,' he said with such assurance that she wondered about the strength of their relationship—and why the woman needed help if it *was* that strong. 'What about counselling her yourself?' he continued. 'You must have done some psychology in your course!'

He was like a summer fly, attacking again and again. She swatted at him, with a quick, 'So must you!'

'But that was so long ago I've forgotten anything I ever knew!' he responded plaintively, forcing her to respond with a dry,

'Poor old thing!' and then to wonder just how old he was! Early thirties, she would guess. . .

Bother the man! He was ruining her walk and disrupting her thoughts, yet her feet moved with a lightness she had not felt for a long time! The track widened and she stepped aside, facing him for the first time this morning, seeing the little lines below the corner of his eyes that crinkled up when he smiled, and the slightly off-centre nose.

'I must speak to each of the others before we get back into town. Please ask your friend—Anne, is it?—to ring the surgery.'

She tried to sound competent, the complete professional, but, glancing quickly up at him and meeting the cool, blue-grey eyes, she felt exactly as he had described her the evening before—like Alice at the bottom of the rabbit hole—alarmed, excited and very definitely apprehensive.

Then he was gone, swinging away in the lead, while she fell in with the next walker, quickly checking the list she was handed of the food he had eaten the previous day.

'Not bad for pre-Christmas, Bob,' she congratulated, 'especially when I know the Volunteer Fire Service party was on last night. You did extremely well!'

'I'm too young to die, Gemma,' he assured her.

'That thought's enough to keep my fingers off the fish and chips!'

He patted her shoulder and moved on, knowing the routine, while she slipped backwards down the line, encouraging, assuring, and occasionally admonishing her little troop as they headed back into the town.

Grant was the last, and he walked with her back to her car.

'Are you bringing that fellow back tonight to repay the dinner?' he asked, and she was startled by the challenge in his voice.

'No way!' she assured him. 'I'm finishing early and going straight home to bed. I've missed enough sleep lately!'

Grant opened the car door for her and held it while she climbed in. 'You do too much,' he said gruffly.

'I'll see you in the morning,' was all she could say, touching his hand in thanks for his apparent concern.

Turning her head to check before backing out of her parking space, she saw Simon Griffiths, leaning against his Range Rover, his head turned towards her, and Grant, his usually mobile face still and watchful.

Anne Kelso came at three. Gemma was surprised to see her, and was uncharacteristically dismayed as she acknowledged the dark beauty and casual sophistication of the woman.

'I'm sorry if I was short with you yesterday,' she greeted her. 'Please sit down and tell me how I can help you.'

'You can't!' was the blunt reply, causing Gemma to put aside all her preconceived notions and to reassess the situation rapidly.

'You're here,' she said gently. 'There must be something I can do.'

'I'm here because Simon insisted, and it's an excuse to get away from the boys.'

'It's hard to keep kids entertained during the holidays,' Gemma sympathised. 'They always seem to have much more energy than their parents.'

'Than this parent, anyway,' the other woman agreed, her fingers moving nervously over her handbag, obviously seeking the solace of a cigarette, yet not daring to produce one. 'Their father could keep up with them! In fact, he could usually tire them out, so that they slept each afternoon and still went to bed early at night.'

Regret was evident in her voice, whether for the absent father or the peaceful days Gemma couldn't tell—but she had her opening.

'Their father couldn't join you these holidays?'

'Their father wouldn't join us!'

Once the words were out in the open, Gemma could sense a slight relaxation in the tension emanating from the woman.

'Too busy at work?' She tempted further confidence.

'Too busy full stop!' came the bitter response. 'How do I know if he's at work? He's got the perfect job for cheating on his wife. A woman rings and asks for him and all he has to say is, "That was Sister Smith from West Wing; I'm needed at the hospital".' She imitated a deep male voice, and took a shuddering breath before continuing, 'And how can I argue? Now, of course, he's got his pager as well. It buzzes and he leaves, just like that. I can't take it! Can't put up with it any more.'

Hysteria edged the words and Gemma's fine-tuned ears picked up a desperation that was deep and genuine. She was trained to respond, and did it automatically, treading with great delicacy into a sphere about which she knew little.

'Is he a specialist that he's called out so often?'

The woman nodded. 'He's an obstetrician and gynaecologist,' she confirmed, 'and seems to be the only one in Melbourne at times. I told him again and again to choose dermatology, or even orthopaedics, like Simon, so we could have a regular life, but no, he had his own ideas!'

'Has it always bothered you—the demands his work puts on him?'

The woman opened her mouth to answer—probably in the affirmative, Gemma guessed—then paused for a moment, and some of the strain slid from her face.

'Not really,' she admitted, after a moment's thought. 'When we first met, I was proud of his dedication, proud that he was determined to do well. Somehow all the studying he did was a joint effort, for both of us. We married while he was still at university.'

A little colour had crept into Anne's pale cheeks, and Gemma watched, fascinated by the visible and audible changes in the woman as she recalled a happier past.

'I worked and kept us both. I felt I was contributing to his success.' And now you feel left out, Gemma wanted to say, but held her tongue, unwilling to stem the flow now that it had begun.

'Even when we had the twins it was easy because, somehow, we shared it all. He was studying for his primaries by that time, and he would do the late-night feeds. He loved the boys—the original besotted father!'

The voice wavered and Gemma reached out and touched one cool hand that now lay, listlessly spent, on the edge of the desk.

'I'm sure he still loves them,' she said.

'He says he does,' their mother remarked, as if surprised that anyone should make such a statement about the two little hellions that were driving her insane. 'But he doesn't seem to show it! Before we separated, he was rarely home, and when he was he complained all the time. They'd be making a dreadful noise, or they'd disobey him, and it was always my fault because I'm not bringing them up properly.'

The words came tumbling out, and with it the resentment and pain.

'It's very easy for the one doing the least to criticise, but, having realised that, it's not as easy to come up with a solution to the problem.'

'I've thought of leaving them with him when he does take his holidays in two weeks' time, and staying up here with Simon,' Anne told her, prompting a quick detouring thought in Gemma's brain. And how long does our Simon take for holidays? She forced her mind back to the problem.

'That might show him how difficult it is for you, trying to bring them up on your own, but your being apart for even longer won't solve your other problems. If you want to try again, to attempt to sort out things between you, it should be done face to face.'

An imp of mischief urged her on.

'Maybe the best idea would be for you to leave the boys with Simon and spend some time alone with your husband. It would give you a chance to talk together.'

'Leave the boys with Simon?' The woman threw back her head and laughed as if Gemma's remark was absolutely hilarious. 'Simon is the world's most confirmed bachelor! He's the original love-'em-and-leave-'em male, absolutely terrified of anything that even hints at commitment! He'll put up with the boys while I'm here to keep him company, but on their own. . .?'

Her voice rose as she considered the absurdity of the situation and Gemma felt distaste shard through her at the image of Simon the woman had projected. And she should know! Gemma admitted bitterly to herself, remembering the pointed 'I'm here to keep him company' remark.

'Perhaps someone else could mind the boys,' she suggested lamely, but she hadn't put Simon completely out of the picture. He professed such great concern for this woman, but was a mite too eager for someone else to be doing all the helping. We'll see about that, she vowed silently, and scribbled her home address on the back of an appointment card.

'It's hard to talk in this place,' she said. 'Why not call and see me at my home this evening? We could have a glass of wine, and you can smoke there if you want to. We'll sit on the veranda and watch the sea, and talk. It might help you sort things out in your own mind,' she added, with a friendly, genuine smile. There was something vulnerable behind the polished façade of Anne Kelso that made Gemma want to help her.

'It would mean getting Simon to mind the boys—that would be twice in one day,' Anne said doubtfully, sounding as if this was a feat beyond all realms of possibility. Gemma pulled out another little card and wrote again.

'Straining the friendship, huh?' she said lightly. 'Here.' She pushed the second card across to Anne. 'There are four teenage girls in this family, all experienced baby-sitters. If you ring, there's sure to be one of them available. If you can't make it this afternoon, then come tomorrow or the next day. I'm usually home by six. I'll get your contact number from your file, and ring if I'm called out.' It was all she could do!

'There's no Mr Wainwright waiting for you?' Anne asked lightly.

'There's no Mr Wainwright,' Gemma confirmed, then wondered why a woman as self-absorbed as Anne was at the moment should have asked such a personal question.

The afternoon patients trekked through, minor holiday problems of sunburn and stomach upsets, another chickenpox—the virus had spread from holiday-makers to the local kids quickly—and then Vicky!

'Not well again, Vick?' Gemma asked sympathetically as the shy teenager edged through the door. In the past three weeks she had treated her for a 'bit of a headache', vague nausea, and unexplained pains in the legs and arms. All on separate occasions, and all, she was certain, not the real reason for the visits.

She had meant to speak to Grant, who was friendly with Vicky's mother. Not to reveal the frequent visits, but to see if she could find out, casually, and without raising suspicions, what might be happening in the young girl's life.

That's another trouble with the long summer holidays, she thought frustratedly. The kids lose that daily contact with each other which is part of their support system. Some go away, others are working, and the grapevine becomes fragmented.

'I'm worried about you, Vicky, love,' she said gently. 'You've had one thing after another this summer. How about I do a full medical, order blood tests——?'

'You did blood tests for the aches and pains. . . thought it might be glandular fever,' the teenager reminded her.

'Well, you're fifteen, the right age for it,' Gemma said as she rifled through the rapidly growing file. 'I probably didn't ask for general tests,' she added, reading quickly through the results from the pathologist to confirm what she was thinking.

Menarche? She'd printed the word on the file twelve months ago and added a question mark. Her eyes slid over the girl's body, noting the small budding breasts and the still childish angularity that should be softening into gentler curves.

'Still waiting for that first period, Vicky?' she asked as casually as she could, knowing that if she touched the wrong nerve the girl would shy away from her, and any hope she had of helping her would be lost.

Colour flooded up under Vicky's dark tan, and Gemma felt a surge of relief. The adolescents she treated came in all shapes and sizes, but all had their own defence mechanisms very securely in place, protecting the fragility of their developing self-esteem. One false move, one rash comment could shatter the precarious trust she was at such pains to build up with them.

'It's not unusual to start late,' she assured her quickly. 'If you feel like talking to your mother about it, you'll probably find she was a late starter as well. The trouble these days is that many girls are actually starting far earlier, which makes the average look late. Does it worry you?'

The dark head bobbed.

'Well, we can't have that at Christmas,' Gemma said lightly. 'There are a few things we could do.'

'Could you put me on the Pill?' The question was asked so eagerly Gemma wondered for a moment about the young girls in this town that she thought she knew. Vicky made being on the Pill sound like some kind of status symbol, but Gemma had prescribed few to young local teenagers, and then only after counselling.

When prescribing it for dysmenorrhoea, or irregularity, she would usually see the girl and a parent, explaining to both what she was doing and why. When a girl was in a steady relationship and wanted it for protection, Gemma persuaded her to bring her boyfriend in as well; that way she could talk to both of them about the hormonal actions that would keep the girl free of unwanted pregnancies, and discuss possible side-effects of long-term use.

'Not immediately,' she replied, covering the surprise and the shadowy disappointment that niggled within her. 'First, we should check and see that there's nothing wrong with your ovaries, which make the eggs and start all the other processes happening.'

She pulled out her trusty diagram of the female reproductive system and showed her young friend precisely what should, and probably soon would, be happening within her body every month.

'Not having periods usually means you're not ovulating, which means your ovaries are not releasing eggs. This could be because they're not ready to yet, or because they have what we call cysts growing there which are blocking things. It's not uncommon, and it's easy to find out, although it means going into Craigstown to see a specialist.'

'Then Mum will have to know?'

'If you're worried about anything, your mum should know,' Gemma said gently. 'She's the best person to confide in because she might have had the same problems herself and can tell you how she got over them.'

'But she's busy with work, and Mark, my little brother, is being a fair devil.'

Gemma grinned. Parents didn't realise how protective of them their kids could be.

'She'd still like you to tell her, I'm sure, or, if you prefer, I can get her to come and see me, and I'll talk to her about it. First, the specialist would do a laparoscopy, which is a simple operation where he makes a tiny slit in your abdomen about here.' She indicated on her own flat stomach. 'He puts an instrument through it that has a light, and he is able to look at your ovaries and see what's going on.'

Vicky's eyes grew round with wonder, and she shifted in her seat as if she could feel the spying instrument already piercing her flesh.

'If there's no obvious problem, then we'll talk about some hormone therapy to jolt your ovaries into action. But first, if you can, talk to your mother. If she started late, you're doing all this worrying for nothing!'

'I will talk to her,' Vicky assured her, committing herself. 'I nearly did a few times and then I thought she'd think I was silly.'

'I think she'll be very pleased to think you are trusting her with your problems and concerns. Ring for another appointment if you both decide to investigate what's happening inside you.'

'Sure will!' said the girl cheerfully, bouncing out of her chair with an energy that Gemma had not seen in her for months.

A tiny shiver of what was almost fear fluttered in Gemma's chest as the vulnerability of adolescence struck her anew. They had to do so much in these years of puberty—decide on vocations, gain independence from their parents, develop their own moral attitudes—and at the same time survive the fads and peer pressures, and the urges towards risk-taking that would lead to independence——

'There's a Simon Griffiths on the phone for you.' Karen's head appeared around the door, interrupting her depressing thoughts, and jolting her back to the present.

'What does he want?'

Karen shrugged expressively. 'He says it's personal!' Heavily pencilled eyebrows rose in a silent question but Gemma ignored it.

'Put him through then send in the next patient when I finish.'

'There's no next patient,' Karen said cheerfully.

'Vicky was the last. Have a chat to your friend and get out of this place while you can!'

'Yes, ma'am!' Gemma replied with a mock-salute, but as the door closed her smile faded and she looked at the telephone with all the wariness of a rabbit watching a fox.

'Are you taking me out to dinner tonight?' His voice sounded deeper on the phone, with a slight huskiness that sent a feather-light touch of apprehension fluttering along her spine.

'I was hoping you'd be minding the boys while I spoke to your friend,' she said coolly. 'She came to see me, but, because it's hard to relax in the surgery atmosphere or to delve very deeply in a short appointment time, I've arranged to see her after work.'

'We've contacted one of the baby-sitters you suggested, so we're both free,' the voice continued, unabashed. 'Anne's seeing you at six then going on to visit friends. I was thinking of after her visit.' There was a short, suggestive pause. 'You do have to eat!' he added persuasively, the words curling into her ear with an insistence she found hard to ignore.

'I also have to sleep,' she said firmly. 'This might be holiday time for ninety per cent of Australia's population, but for the other ten per cent it's the busiest time of the year.'

'Tomorrow night?' he asked hopefully and she could almost believe he was pleading with her. There was something incongruous about this, she decided, but his presence was too close, reverberating through the wires into the privacy of her office, for her to analyse the incongruity.

'Or better still,' he was saying, 'I'll bring something over tonight, then we can have a quick meal together and you can still have an early night.'

'I thought I owed *you* dinner,' she replied, playing

for time while her brain tried to think. She knew she should say no, or at least argue a little more, but the temptation to see him again, to talk to someone who understood her work and could share her problems, overwhelmed the doubts—and her usually strong common sense.

'I'll let you pay,' he offered generously, and the teasing lilt in his voice brought his face, creased into a smile, so vividly to mind that she smiled back into the phone.

'OK,' she agreed weakly. 'But you'd better leave it until eight, or you'll be meeting Anne on my doorstep, and that might complicate your simple life.'

'I detect a note of censure in your soft voice, Doctor, dear,' he murmured, sending a heated tide of blood into Gemma's cheeks. 'The relationship between myself and Anne is purely that of old and trusted friends, supporting each other in our hours of need.'

'Hours of need, indeed!' Gemma snorted. 'Anne may be having problems, which you seem to be handling quite admirably. . .' she paused '. . .by passing them on to me, but you didn't strike me as a person bowed down by worry or sorrow.'

'That's only because you don't know me at all well,' he told her plaintively, then added the final warning, 'Yet!' and hung up.

Gemma held the receiver up in front of her, looking at it with a mesmeric fascination. He was flirting with her, she knew—and laying down a challenge! She wasn't a rabbit watching a fox, she decided, but a weasel, hypnotised by a snake-charmer's cobra. She coiled the handpiece in front of her, acting out the little fantasy, while her mind followed the thought further.

It wasn't the snake she feared, she acknowledged with a shudder as she replaced the receiver in its cradle, but the charmer! And do I fear him, or the potency of his charms? she asked herself. Do I fear the present, which excites me with its offer of some pleasant dalliance, or the future, which may be doubly bleak when he is gone?

It was nearly three years since she had returned to Grange Bay, four years since she had realised that she and Alex must go their separate ways. The long hours of work—as an intern, a locum and finally here, when she set up the practice—had exhausted her body, while the often daunting challenges of each new step along her chosen career path had kept her mind free from concern about the future.

Until recently! Now she was settled back into the security of her old home town and had achieved an easy regularity in her job, but somehow the satisfaction she had expected to feel, and did experience from time to time, was not as fulfilling as she had imagined it would be. The pressures had eased, and, with that easing, she had begun to sense something lacking in her busy life.

Without admitting to loneliness, she was still aware that her mind needed someone to share her thoughts, and, worse still, she had begun to suspect that her body was beginning to need someone to share her bed. Try as she might to rationalise her thoughts and feelings, the physical symptoms remained, and there were times when she ached for a man's arms around her, a deep voice in her ear.

But Simon Griffiths is not the man, she argued fiercely with herself. He's just passing through! A holiday romance that will set the town's collective tongues wagging and leave you lonelier than ever! There's no future in it, she warned herself, then smiled as all her caution and common sense were swamped by an irrational delight. She would see him tonight!

CHAPTER FOUR

LAST night it had been Simon bounding up the steps as she'd shut the surgery door behind her, but tonight it was a tired, harassed-looking young mother, holding a limply quiet infant in her arms. And she dragged herself up, rather than bounded!

Disappointment flared as professionalism warred with personal desires. Gemma had hoped to have time to shower and change then relax for a while before Anne Kelso arrived. She'd thought about washing her hair—but whether for Anne or Simon she refused to consider!

She watched the woman pull herself carefully up towards her, and sighed. Then, with a bright smile, she pushed the door back open and motioned this one last patient through the deserted waiting-room and into her office.

The baby's skin was dry and hot, his eyes sunken, his pulse tumultuous. She pinched his wrist and saw the skin stand where she had left it, and her heart sank.

'He's dehydrated,' she said, debating whether he should be sent off to hospital in Craigstown where a drip would restore both fluid and electrolyte balance or if she could get sufficient fluids back into him without it. 'Are you still breast-feeding him?'

She reached into her sample cupboard for a sachet of Gastrolyte as she spoke, and poured it into a jug, mixing sterile water from a silver flask into the crystalline powder.

'No,' the woman replied. 'He's eight months old and I weaned him before we came on holidays. He's been taking the bottle well, but yesterday we stopped at a motel for the night, and he didn't seem to want it. He'd been a bit sick and I thought it was because of the car journey. He had slight diarrhoea, and today—well, he's been that quiet, I didn't bother much. He did have half a bottle of juice this morning.'

'We'll try this in a bottle first,' Gemma said reassuringly to the tearful young woman, rummaging in her 'everything' cupboard for a bottle and teat, and pouring a little of the pale, glucose-rich mixture into it.

The baby grizzled fretfully, closing his lips against the invading teat. Showing total uninterest in the unappetising mixture, he turned his head against his mother, and whimpered fractiously. Gemma poured the mixture from the bottle into a cup then sat down beside them and took the baby on to her knee.

'We'll do it the slow way then, little man,' she said calmly, taking a teaspoon and spooning some into his mouth. He gagged and choked, but most of it slid down. Then the little lips clamped tightly shut, and she had to force them open with her thumb against his cheek, easing his chin up at the same time to force him to swallow.

'It's not easy to make him take it, but it must be done,' she told the distressed mother. She spooned more in, fighting the squirming, whimpering infant but still murmuring quietly and soothingly as she pressed the liquid through his resisting lips.

'He's got to have fluids whether he feels like it or not,' she explained, 'especially in the summer, and when you're travelling. The heat in the car promotes dehydration.'

'I did know that,' the young woman confessed, 'but the other two were playing up and he was being so good!'

Because he was half dead, Gemma felt like saying but she held her tongue and kept spooning.

'Are you stopping here or going further on?' she asked, considering her next move.

'We're only going this far. My husband's mum and dad live here—Mary and Dave Parsons. I'm married to Bill.'

I went to school with Bill, Gemma thought as the woman's light voice continued her explanations, and here he is with three kids! Another pin-prick of unease! A sense of time passing!

'Bill dropped me here and took the other two on to his mum. He'll come back for me and the baby.'

The anxiety was disappearing from her voice, and Gemma sensed that the horror of that long, hot trip with three young children in the car was slowly fading.

'Do you think he'll be sick for long?' she asked, as if anxious that it might spoil their holiday plans.

'He shouldn't be,' Gemma assured her. 'I want you to keep him on the Gastrolyte for twenty-four hours. I'll give you another two sachets, one for later tonight and one for tomorrow morning. You can get some more from the chemist when he opens at nine, and try to get a full 200mls into him every four hours during the day. You can offer him unsweetened diluted juice as well, but no milk or solids until his intestines have had time to sort themselves out.'

'But if he won't take it in a bottle, it'll take all day to feed him,' the young woman objected, her naturally casual approach to life returning now she was reassured that her baby would not die.

'Mary and Dave will both help,' Gemma said firmly. 'If you feel you can't do it, I would have to put him into hospital over in Craigstown, and you'd be stuck there with him while Bill and the kids enjoyed their holiday.'

'Oh!' said the girl, startled as much by the sudden coolness in Gemma's voice as by her warning words.

'It's absolutely essential that you get the fluid into him,' Gemma repeated. 'Dehydration causes a build-up of salt in the body which can cause major problems like kidney failure. With babies the risk is much higher, especially in summer, when they should be drinking more fluids, not less.'

She looked at the container and judged that, while she talked, she'd got at least 100 mls into the little body. Could she trust the mother to see that he got the rest? It was five-thirty. If she left now, she could hurry home and still have time to shower and change before Anne was due; then at least she'd be clean when Simon arrived.

She shook her head slightly, as if to dispel a thought that was so uncharacteristic it was unbelievable, and went on spooning, knowing she would be negligent to let the child go before his first lot of fluid was safely inside him.

Anne was on the veranda, smoking and looking out over the town towards the sea.

'I'm sorry I'm late,' Gemma apologised. 'One last patient turned up as I shut the door! Would you like a cool drink?'

'A glass of wine would be nice,' Anne responded, her eyes still on the view and her thoughts far-away.

Unlocking the door, Gemma walked through the hot, stuffy house, throwing open windows to allow the cooling breeze to flow through. She dropped her bag on the kitchen table and washed her hands at the sink, thinking regretfully of the shower she could not take until later.

'I don't know much about wine,' she confessed, handing Anne a glass, and motioning her towards a comfortable deckchair. 'People give me a bottle now and then. I usually have one in the refrigerator, in case I feel like a glass with my dinner, but I'm hardly a connoisseur.'

'Tastes fine to me!' Anne responded politely, but Gemma sensed a withdrawal and wondered why she had become involved in the woman's problems. She did not have the training to help her. If they were friends, it would be different, she thought, because women friends provided a natural support network around each other.

'I don't think you can help,' Anne said suddenly, putting into words what Gemma had been thinking, but adding a shade of what was almost rudeness.

'No,' Gemma agreed, 'but if you want to talk I can listen. Sometimes your own friends can be too close to the situation to see it clearly, and often there are things you can say to a stranger that you can't tell your friends.'

There was another silence, and Gemma sipped at her orange juice, feeling tension building up inside her at a time when it was usually draining out.

'It's all to do with my smoking, you know!'

The statement was delivered flatly, and Gemma recognised it as part of the truth. It matched the defiant flourish with which Anne lit cigarettes, and the deliberate exhalation of the smoke.

'Has your husband given up?'

'Yes!' An angry affirmative. 'And he says it's easy! I stopped when I was pregnant and he kept smoking. Right up till the boys were nearly three, I stayed off. Then they both had some infection and were sick for ages, and Jake was studying, so I started again and he stopped and it's the one thing he always picks on when we argue.'

Now is not the time to suggest she should give up,

Gemma decided, pleased that Anne was talking but floundering in her own role as counsellor.

'Are the boys at school yet?' she asked, thinking that discussion of a neutral topic might ease the tension she could hear rising in Anne's voice.

'No, they're still at pre-school and that's only three days a week.'

'Which means you have them at home most of the time, at precisely the age when they need more and more stimulation,' Gemma said sympathetically. 'I often wonder how mothers manage to survive those early years with their kids. It's no wonder you feel you need the soothing effects of a cigarette even if the rotten things are bad for your health.'

'Are they as bad as everyone says?' Anne asked quickly, sensing an ally. 'Both my parents have smoked all their lives and they're still fit and healthy.'

'They might be the lucky ones,' Gemma replied sombrely. 'Unfortunately, the more research that is done, the more harmful side-effects are discovered. Now the scientists are looking at it increasing the effects of ageing on the skin. More wrinkles and earlier!' Gemma shuddered realistically. 'As if we women don't have enough to worry about!'

'If it's that bad, I might have to take to the bottle instead!' Anne drained her glass.

'Or try to sort out things between yourself and your husband. Your support should come from him, not artificial stimulants,' Gemma said quietly, hoping she wouldn't kill the rapport that was developing between them.

'Yes,' Anne agreed, in a voice that said such a solution might not be possible.

'But it's got to be what you both want, this marriage. It's not enough, in any relationship, for one partner to always be the one trying to make things work.'

'That's happened to you?' Anne looked for a common bond.

'No!' Gemma had to tell her, knowing that her own relationship had broken up because of different ideals, and widely divergent visions of the future. 'But I have seen many instances where it fell to one person to look after the emotional well-being of the partnership. I think I can understand.'

Anne stubbed out a half-smoked cigarette and stood up. While Gemma waited in a silence that was no longer taut, she walked across and leaned against the veranda railing. Her eyes were on the distant horizon but her thoughts could have been anywhere.

'But what can I do?' she asked at last.

'Decide what you want for yourself, and your future—apart from the needs of your husband, children, everything else!' Gemma told her bluntly. 'You've got to regain your own sense of identity first. Make goals for yourself, then work out how they can be fulfilled within your marriage.'

She looked across at Anne, who was still staring out to sea, and sensed that she was listening carefully.

'I know it sounds like all the old psychological hype, but it amounts to doing whatever you can to take control of your own life, to stop being carted along on currents that are formed solely from the needs of others.'

Anne nodded, and continued her study of the sea, and Gemma felt the peace of her home begin to work its usual magic. She might not have helped much, but she was reasonably certain that she had done no harm.

'It seems easy when you think it through.'

'And it's far easier to say than to do,' Gemma agreed, the sympathy she felt for the woman deepening her voice, 'but sometimes starting is the hardest part.'

'Simon said you'd understand. He said you had wise eyes.'

And what on earth did he mean by that? Gemma wondered, trying to ignore a tiny spurt of delight at the unexpected compliment.

'I've got to go,' Anne said finally, and Gemma rose to walk with her to her car. 'I'll think about what you said. May I come again?'

'Any time,' Gemma assured her. 'Ring first to make sure I'm here.'

She watched the car disappear back down the hill towards the town, then hurried back inside. A shower was essential, she decided, feeling the tacky stickiness of a long, hot day, compounded by spilt Gastrolyte. Simon could entertain himself for a short time if necessary!

His footsteps echoed from the veranda as she was drying herself, and she called out for him to come in, to make himself at home. Then, with fingers that trembled slightly, she smoothed cream into her skin, before slipping into a cool cotton sundress.

'There's wine or beer in the refrigerator,' she told him, opening the bathroom door to call through to him as she brushed her hair.

'I've brought my own supply,' the deep voice answered, 'and I'll wait for you to share it with me.'

Again, a quivering feeling of excitement unsettled Gemma's composure. The face reflected in the bathroom mirror seemed lit by an inner radiance that neither doubts nor common sense could diminish.

Honestly, she chided the excited image, you'd think you'd never had a date before in your entire life. Her fingers pulled the shining length of her hair through a narrow band, then twisted the tail until it coiled into a firm knot on the top of her head. She ran two pins into the knot to keep it secure, added some mascara, lipstick and a quick dusting of powder, and emerged to greet her neglected guest.

He stood against the railing where Anne had stood a short time earlier, looking out to sea.

'It weaves a magic spell, this view of yours,' he said in his deep, even voice, then he turned and smiled at her. 'Well, well! Sophisticated Alice tonight!' he added, taking in the upswept hair, then allowing his gaze to slide slowly down over her body with an appreciative quirking of his lips.

I can't handle this! she thought as panic and excitement churned her insides to a totally unfamiliar turbulence. She nodded acknowledgement of his compliment with a masking and totally false aplomb.

'I brought champagne,' he added, with a smile that invited her to join him in some sybaritic indulgence. 'I realise you can't have much to drink, and I have to drive home later, so I thought we might as well enjoy a little of the best.'

He waved a hand towards the low table between her deckchairs, and she was astonished to see a silver ice-bucket with a bottle of champagne protruding from a nest of ice. He'd brought the meal, the wine, and also the necessary props! This was not a casual take-away meal, but serious seduction, she decided, steeling herself to handle whatever might lie ahead with some degree of composure.

'Not French?' she asked lightly, knowing that the local pub did not run to such luxuries.

'Of course!' he replied, bowing slightly, his eyes catching hers with a mocking, taunting gleam.

She stayed away from him, pretending a casualness she was far from feeling as she settled herself into a chair and admired the arrangement of food on the table beside her.

'I've never tasted it,' she told him calmly, trying to

bring the situation under control with some matter-of-fact conversation.

'Well, tonight's the night! And with it we have, for starters, some pâté, King Island Brie and Camembert, fresh prawns with avocado, and oysters.'

He walked across and stood beside her, waving his hand above the plate of nibbles, as he pointed out the special culinary delights.

'For starters? That sounds more like a full meal!' she protested, her heart skipping at his nearness while her mind tried to pretend disinterest.

'Fresh crab salad for main course and mango mousse and ice-cream to finish up.' He reached for the champagne and removed the gold foil and twisted wire as he spoke. 'Does it meet with madam's approval?' The subdued popping of the cork punctuated the question.

'You haven't found this menu in any take-away place in Grange Bay,' Gemma declared, shaking her head in disbelief.

'I found all the ingredients,' he assured her, pouring a glass of the sparkling wine and bending towards her. 'It's a town of hidden treasures,' he added, handing her the glass and looking down into her eyes with a teasing glimmer of laughter.

Why has he chosen me for his holiday fling? Gemma wondered desperately. With my erratic hours, I must be the least accessible woman in town!

'Don't look so worried, Alice,' he murmured in a husky whisper. 'Rabbit burrows have many exits.'

'I'm more bemused than worried,' she said, marvelling at the even tenor of her voice as she tried to divert his interest from personal back to professional. 'It's a long time since anyone flirted with me. In fact,' she added with what she hoped was disarming candour, 'I can't understand why anyone would want to—especially at this time of the year when I'm on call twenty-four hours a day and usually working at least twelve of them.'

'Could it be that I find you different?' he replied, the hint of laughter that seemed such an integral part of him lightening his voice. He sliced a piece of cheese and spread it carefully on a biscuit, his eyes on what he was doing but his body bombarding hers with unspoken messages.

'Very different, I would imagine, from your usual run of sophisticated city beauties,' she retorted, sipping at the sparkling wine, and concentrating on the sensation of the tiny bubbles fizzing against her tongue. 'Do you feel the need for a little variety?'

Gemma spoke quickly, hoping that the light, bantering tone of her conversation would keep her more insidious thoughts and feelings at bay.

'Try this!' was his only response. He proffered the biscuit, moving it not towards her fingers, clinging to the stem of her champagne flute, but towards her lips, which parted to receive the tasty morsel. She bit into the biscuit and chewed, aware of his eyes on her face, his fingers close to her mouth, his body hovering beside her chair.

'Good?' he asked and brushed his thumb across her lips as if to gather a last neglected crumb.

She nodded, unable to trust her voice as this man wove his spell of sensual mastery round her, insinuating his potent chemistry into every cell in her body with an ease that shook her.

I know what he's doing, she thought desperately, so why can't I resist it? It seemed as if she was splitting into two people; one the practical, efficient young doctor, secure in her town and her career, the other a stranger she did not know, who wanted to throw off the cloak of respectable responsibility and dance to the tune of this charmer for a little while.

'Would it be so wrong?' he asked, bringing her back out of her meandering mind with her own question.

'Wrong?' She looked up into his eyes.

'To flirt with you?' He smiled his lazy smile and moved away, but hardly far enough to ease the surging turbulence his closeness had evoked.

'No,' she said carefully, 'but highly inpractical.' She was pleased that she sounded far calmer than she felt. 'People on holidays should play with other holiday-makers and let the locals get on with their jobs. Speaking of which——' His eyebrow rose questioningly, and she added, 'My job,' very firmly before continuing, 'I spoke to Anne this afternoon but I think she needs professional help—they both do—if the marriage is to succeed.'

'Diverting the conversation back to neutral ground?' he asked mockingly, easing himself down into the chair on the other side of the small table.

'Most definitely,' she responded, impaling a succulent prawn on a toothpick and lifting it to her lips. 'You bribed me with food—which I would like to pay for, by the way—and with the added enticement of the companionship of a colleague. That's the reason you're here.' She spoke severely.

'Keep to medical topics or go home?'

He was challenging her to deny that she was enjoying his company, to declare that her only interest in him was purely professional. That gauntlet could lie where it was thrown, she decided.

'Not till we've finished these and tried your crab salad,' she returned, picking up another biscuit and adding cheese. 'It's a local crab, I hope?'

'Most certainly. I had thought, until yesterday, that it was the greatest attraction of Grange Bay—the wealth of fresh seafood your trawlers bring in each morning.'

She could feel his eyes on her, but ignored the far from subtle compliment hidden in his words.

'But every seaside town along the coast has its fishing fleet. That can't be what's bringing you southerners flocking to the town.' Tourism provided a diversion, and she pursued the subject in a desultory fashion as the tension of the day drained away.

'It's a beautiful, peaceful little haven, Gemma. Isn't that enough appeal?'

'For some people, yes,' she conceded. 'But those people have been coming here for years and years. It's all you new tourists that make me suspicious.'

'Sweeping in to buy up the town and turn it into a mega-resort?'

'It's happened before in other places,' she argued.

'I'm not a millionaire developer in disguise as an over-worked orthopod,' he assured her with a deep chuckle. 'Is it hunger that's making you argumentative?'

'Me argumentative? I like that. You started arguing with me before we'd even met, attacking my professionalism on my own front steps.'

'For which I now apologise most sincerely,' he said in humble submission. 'If I'd thought it through, I'd have realised Anne's version of events would be highly coloured—not that you failed to put me right immediately. Maybe it was that unexpectedly fiery spirit in one so meek and mild in looks that stole my heart.'

He spoke the words in his usual lazy drawl, his eyes fixed on some point on the far horizon, but Gemma felt an impact in them that she did not want to admit to.

'Now that you've managed to turn the conversation back from your aggressive behaviour to flirting, maybe we'd better eat,' she said severely, hoping she could keep some kind of control over the situation.

'Eat we shall, little coward,' he assured her, making it clear that he was still following her thoughts with his uncanny percipience. 'Inside or out?'

'Inside, I think,' she answered quickly, hoping that electric light would dispel some of his charm, and that a solid table between them would ease her quivering senses.

How much of her house had he explored while she'd showered? He led the way with a strange familiarity into her kitchen, and waved his hand towards the small dining-table, already set with unfamiliar place-mats and cutlery.

'Some service!' she admitted, shaking her head admiringly as he produced food from the refrigerator and served her with all the aplomb of a head waiter pandering to the needs of a favoured customer.

'We aim to please,' he said easily, taking his place opposite her at the table and smiling disarmingly.

I know you're just as dangerous when you're playing this part, she wanted to say, but confined herself to remarks about the weather and the state of the surf, usually favoured topics with all visitors.

'And no, I don't fish,' he said as they finished their meal and sat back to savour the pleasant feeling of repletion.

Puzzled, she looked across the table and caught the teasing gleam in his eyes.

'Wouldn't that have been the next question?'

'Probably!' she admitted, but refused to give up the slight advantage she had gained. 'Do you walk?' she asked instead. 'There are some great walks in the national park to the north and west of here.'

'I don't walk either! Well, not much!' He had rested his elbows on the table and now leaned forward, cupping his chin in his hands and gazing steadfastly into her eyes.

Refusing to be intimidated, Gemma continued to probe—talking about him kept the dangers of his indisputable physical attraction at bay!

'Then why choose Grange Bay?' she asked. 'Victoria has its own surf beaches, although the weather would be colder. Or there are all the better-known tourist spots further north and south of here. They cater for city tourists, with better shopping, and more restaurants, golf courses, night-clubs and even theme parks.'

'Gemma Wainwright!' he exclaimed in tones of great disbelief. 'Do I look like a man who needs constant entertainment? Wild nightlife? Man-made pleasures?'

'Yes,' she pronounced with great seriousness. 'You do!'

'You'll have to explain that,' he warned, and she shifted in her seat, then reached forward and picked up her wine glass, to drain the last few drops. That done, settling her elbows comfortably on the table, she confronted him.

'You look like a man of elegant tastes——'

'You're guessing on the basis of the wine, not looks!' he argued.

'Looks!' she reiterated firmly, refusing to be put off. 'You've got the sort of face I see all the time in the social pages of magazines, smiling lazily above an immaculate dinner-jacket and bow-tie, with a dazzling beauty attached to your arm like a limpet. Dr Griffiths and friend at the opera. Dr Griffiths escorted Lady Flub to the gala dinner!'

'I would never take Lady Flub to dinner,' he protested in accents of mock-horror, and they both laughed.

'You're partly right,' he admitted, his face now serious as he looked around her big open room, then back at her face, her eyes. 'But isn't all that frantic social activity enough excuse to find a quiet haven like Grange Bay for my holidays?'

Now there was a seriousness behind the laughter.

'I don't know,' she said honestly.

'You could find out,' he responded so softly that she wondered if she had actually heard the words.

Raising her eyes to search his face, she caught a kind of tenderness in his expression, and felt an almost suffocating clenching of muscles in her chest, as if a giant hand were squeezing the air from her lungs.

'I don't want a holiday romance with you,' she whispered, shaking her head. 'I'm too busy and too tired and too settled, and I don't want it!'

There was a quiet desperation in the words that came tumbling out, as if she was denying herself, not him—denying something he hadn't yet suggested!

He smiled at her then—a lazy, gentle, teasing, sensuous smile that melted her bones and made her stomach plummet.

'Methinks the lady. . .' he murmured, and reached across the table to touch her hand. 'I promised you an early night,' he added almost abruptly, his eyes gleaming with secret messages which she could no longer interpret.

Gemma nodded, wondering how she could possibly sleep when her body was alive with a tingling awareness of its needs, and her mind was a whirling mass of confusion.

To her surprise, he pushed back his chair and rose to his feet, lifting the dirty crockery off the table as he moved. Without another word, he started packing empty containers and dirty dishes into a large wicker picnic basket.

'Rub the lamp once and the genie will disappear!' he told her, his voice deep and oddly serious.

'You're mixing your fairy-stories now,' she warned,

hoping to hide the contrary sense of disappointment she was feeling.

'Variety is the spice of life, remember.' He winked and closed the top of the basket, then hefted it into the air and walked towards the front door.

Was he really leaving as uncomplainingly as this? Gemma wondered, rising rather shakily to her feet and following him on to the veranda where he was gathering up the last of his belongings.

Watching his neat, deft movements, she could imagine him in Theatre, operating with an economic efficiency. This vivid image of him at work added another dimension to his undeniable attraction.

He finished his cleaning up, and straightened to look down at her.

'You look as if you're wondering whether to rub the lamp or not, Doctor, dear,' he said, a note of warning in his voice.

'I'm going to rub,' she told him quickly. 'I need a good night's sleep!'

'Then you shall have it!' he replied, and, before she realised what he was doing, he reached out and took her gently by the shoulders, and bent to plant a friendly kiss firmly on her lips. 'I'll be in touch,' he said, lifting his basket, and striding off the veranda, to disappear from view into her mini-jungle.

She did not follow, but moved slowly across to the railing, to lean against it, looking out over the blue-black sea. She heard a car door slam, an engine fire, and the quiet scrunching of the tyres as it glided down the hill.

'He's bewitching me,' she told the balmy summer night air.

CHAPTER FIVE

SIMON was at the beach again next morning, and Gemma felt her stomach flip as she recognised his tall, strong frame among the cluster of walkers. The night had brought no counsel, for she had slept from the moment she closed her eyes until the alarm aroused her in the morning.

Some time today, she promised herself, I'll sit and think about all this.

She waved her arm in the air for the group to follow and set off down the beach. There was a sullen swell far out to sea, and the waves curling on to the shore were higher and more forceful than the previous day. Signs of a low wind far off the north Queensland coast, she thought as her eyes, trained from childhood to observe the sea in all its moods, unconsciously noted the changes.

'That coming for you?' Bob, who was head of the local volunteer fire service, had been walking beside her, and his ears had picked up the loud vibrating roar of the helicopter engine seconds before she recognised its noisy beat.

It floated down to rest on the headland in front of them, like some misshapen insect settling on a leaf. The group moved on towards it.

The helicopter was funded by local businesses in five coastal towns, and was used for search and rescue missions, shark-spotting, and emergency airlifts. Gemma watched Ian Wilson, one of the volunteer observers in the craft, duck under the decelerating rotors and hurry towards them.

'We need you, Gemma,' he called. 'There's been an accident out on the *Frantic Fan* and the ambulance boys were called to a pile-up on the highway.'

'Do you know what's happened?' She was aware of the little group pressing closer; aware, also, of the stranger in their midst!

'Fellow crushed his leg. Seems the net drum slipped and caught him. New young chap Sam took on for the holidays.'

'You've got the emergency kit on board?' she asked as she followed him back towards the helicopter. She could feel the blood draining out of her body and forced herself to act normally. It had to happen some time, she supposed—an emergency call to a trawler.

'Sure have, but we do need someone with the nous to use it,' Ian was saying cheerfully, unaware of her reaction to his news.

'How many will the chopper hold?'

Gemma spun around. Simon was right behind her, with Grant by his side.

'Seven at a pinch—five and two stretchers,' Ian answered automatically, evidently recognising some authority in Simon's voice.

'I'll come with you; I've New South Wales registration,' Simon said, touching Gemma on the arm. 'If the limb has been crushed, you'll be dealing with a comminuted fracture and all the associated damage to tissues, blood vessels and nerves. We might be able to stabilise him and then minimise further damage if I look at it before he's shifted.'

Gemma nodded. What he said made sense. Could she let him go on his own? The treacherous thought barely surfaced before it was thrust away.

'Will you be OK?' Grant was beside her, his arm around her shoulder, and she turned towards him and nodded, then saw the concern and sympathy in the eyes of his fellow walkers. They all knew how she was feeling!

She ducked and ran towards the little bug that would lift them into the air and swing them out across the water, then drop them, like pieces of baggage, on to the pitching wooden deck of a fish trawler, out beyond the horizon.

Simon passed her and swung into the cabin, reaching down to pull her up. He watched as she pulled on a life-jacket and strapped herself in, then he followed her actions carefully. Ian passed them each a set of earphones. Kim Ryan, the pilot, greeted her warmly as they lifted off, and explained where they were going. Gemma introduced Simon.

'Been dropped before?' Kim asked him.

'Never even flown in one of these contraptions,' he responded cheerfully.

'Well, the procedure's simple,' Kim explained. 'You'll be attached to the cable by that quick-release buckle on the front of your life-jacket. There's a loop at the end of your foot, and if you hang on you'll find it easier for balance. Got that?'

Simon repeated the instructions, smiling at the competence of the young girl who was piloting them with such skill.

'We winch you down,' she continued. 'All you do is hang there, then, when you're on your feet, hit the release buckle and move clear of the cable. If you bend your knees as you come towards the deck of the boat, it'll lessen the impact of your touchdown. Don't need a broken ankle to complicate things, do we?'

'I shall do my best,' Simon promised seriously.

'You'll be all right, Gemma,' Kim said reassuringly as the fishing fleet came into view below them. 'Just remember, it's not like dropping on to rocks, because the deck will be moving. Sam and the boys will grab you, and the gear. The two-way's in the emergency kit—I checked it myself—and you've three units of plasma in case there are any problems and you need to stabilise him before you shift him. I'll go back to Grange and wait till I hear from you, OK?'

'If the ambulance is at a road accident, it'll be ferrying patients on from there to Craigstown, and won't be back for some time. Even if we bring him in on the boat, we'll probably need you to take him into town.' Gemma's mind raced ahead, trying to overcome problems that might arise in the transfer of the injured man.

'That's what I figured,' Kim agreed. 'Sam reckons they're about three-quarters of an hour out, and he'll keep steaming towards home. I'll wait by the wharf. We'll drop you first,' she added as they swooped low over the brightly painted trawler and acknowledged the waving crew, 'then the stretcher, then the big guy. Good luck!' she added as Gemma edged out of her seat and into the back of the cabin, automatically readying herself for the descent.

Once she was winched down, Sam's big arms caught and held her tight for a fraction of a second.

'You had to come back some day, girl,' he said brusquely, then led her across the deck to where the injured deckhand lay.

'He's made a right mess of his leg and lost a lot of blood,' he said worriedly. 'We've stopped the bleeding, but I had to use a tourniquet, which I don't like, but I didn't dare put a pressure bandage on in case I made the mess of crushed bone worse!'

'Is it just his leg that's injured?' Gemma asked. 'What happened?'

Sam explained how the cable had twisted on the drum, and the young lad, with more enthusiasm than experience, had tried to free it, but instead had released the brake and brought the heavy drum back down on his leg.

'You've done well, Sam,' Gemma reassured him as she knelt and felt for a pulse in the cold, clammy arm of the young man, at the same time lifting one eyelid to check dilation of the pupil. He was semi-conscious, his body having provided its own relief mechanism in reaction to the pain and shock.

Two young men arrived with the stretcher and, strapped to it, the medical-emergency kit kept on the helicopter. Opening it, Gemma fitted a stethoscope to her ears, and bent to shift the blanket and unbutton the lad's shirt.

'Into impending shock, is he?' Simon asked, squatting beside her and releasing the tourniquet while his eyes assessed the damage to the leg.

'I'd say so,' Gemma said quietly as she listened to the heartbeat. 'There's sinus tachycardia and an atrial rate of a hundred and ten beats a minute.' She unstrapped the OxyViva that was attached to the lightweight, moulded stretcher and fitted the mask carefully to the young man's face, pressing it down to ensure a good seal. Adjusting the controls to a flow of eight litres per minute, she checked the demand valve, and watched the blue tinge fade from his lips as the concentrated oxygen eased his air hunger and hyperventilation. 'I'll start him on plasma.'

Talking all the time—explaining every step of what she was doing—she reached again into the kit, found a squashy fluid reservoir, and checked it carefully—plasma, ready for immediate use. Butterfly needles for insertion into a vein and sterilised tubing were in sealed plastic bags, all labelled, and complete with precise instructions. She pulled on a pair of gloves and worked quickly, breaking seals and assembling what she would need.

Connecting the tube to the reservoir, she flushed the tube with the clear liquid, and checked the flow-rate printed on the pack. Holding the young man's arm, she tied the blood-pressure bandage around it, and applied pressure to raise a vein in the back of his hand, then inserted the short metal needle and stabilised it with the plastic tabs. Releasing the tourniquet, she attached the tube to the needle and began the infusion by opening the clamp again.

Delving into the bag once more, she produced tape and scissors and taped the needle securely into place, before looping the tube and taping it as well.

'You sit and hold this,' she said to the young crew member who hovered over them, clearly concerned for his friend. 'You might as well be useful,' she added as she lowered her head over the stethoscope and listened again to the erratic beating of the youth's labouring heart.

'How are you going?' Simon asked as she raised her head again. 'Can we lift him on to the stretcher? I've got an air splint of sorts under the leg, but I'd rather immobilise this leg *in situ* than start now and then move him again.'

'I'm ready,' she agreed, still watching anxiously as the cyanosis of the youth's finger nails faded to a healthier but still pale pink. She diluted the oxygen he was breathing slightly. 'Just rest that bag on his chest and help lift him when we tell you,' she told the helper.

Simon had prepared the stretcher, spreading out the straps and space blanket, and placing gauze pads in position where the injured leg would rest. He gave his instructions clearly and concisely, and, again, Gemma told the stirring patient what they were doing as they lifted him in one easy movement on to the stretcher.

As Gemma wrapped the patient, adjusted the straps,

fixed the oxygen cylinder in place and checked the vital signs again, Simon continued working on the leg.

'Has he stabilised?' he asked, his attention still focused on the leg.

'Yes, at the moment,' Gemma told him. 'How's the leg?'

'I'd like to give him a pain-killer and then try to move the bone. I think it's still compressing the blood vessels and nerves and we'll get more permanent damage if I can't release that pressure.'

'They have morphine in the kit. I'll start him with 5mg, in case it makes him sick,' Gemma agreed, glad that she did not have to deal with the additional problem of the wound. Stabilising patients for transport to hospital had been the main focus of her emergency work in recent years, and she had tried not to think about what extra help she might have been able to give them had she been more skilled. She injected the narcotic into the thigh muscle of his good leg, and turned to Simon, offering help.

'Now, if you can irrigate the wound for me while I have a look,' Simon told her, handing her a bag of saline solution he had found in the medical kit. She moved to squat beside him, and saw, for the first time, the extent of the damage.

The heavy chain had caught the young man's leg and dragged it down and under the drum, causing ugly flesh wounds, as well as the fractured bones and torn blood vessels. A tourniquet had been the only way to stop the bleeding, and Simon had replaced it with a pressure cuff, inflated to restrict the blood flow. Every minute it was in place, there was a danger of further damage to the distal part of the leg.

It was evident from the blood still seeping from the wound that Simon was adjusting it regularly, but as she surveyed the damage and obeyed Simon's instructions it seemed to Gemma that there was little hope of saving the lower extremity of the limb.

Beneath her feet the throbbing note of the engine changed, and she realised they were coming into the mouth of the river, and would soon be tied up at the jetty. She hadn't contacted Kim, but knew she would be waiting. Even with her mind wholly concentrated on the job she was doing, Gemma felt the familiar rhythms of the boat, and knew an inner gladness that she had finally broken an old spell. Ten years since she'd been on a trawler. Ten years since —

'I'll go into the chopper with him,' Simon said suddenly, bringing her back to the present with a thud. 'I don't want to splint this any more, or do anything that will have to be undone when he gets to town. If there's a theatre available and we can get him straight in, I think we might still save the leg.'

Gemma heard an excitement in his voice and knew he saw it as a challenge. With that thought came another—more a certainty than idle speculation: challenge was something this man would thrive on. Was she a challenge to him, or just a diversion?

That she could even think of something so personal at a time like this shocked her. Where was the cool professional who took such pride in all her work?

'I'll phone ahead and let them know what's happening and what we've done,' she told Simon, trying to appear calmly competent. 'Any special needs?'

'Better not say too much,' he said with a conspiratorial smile. 'I'll have to be careful not to tread on any toes. I'll go with him and hang around, hoping someone will ask me to help.'

'If it was a bad accident on the highway, they are probably flat out and will welcome you with open arms.'

'Which is more than some of their colleagues do,' he

murmured, his fingers still lifting scraps of bone from the mangled cavity, and his eyes following them intently.

'We'll take him now!' Ian was by their side, and Gemma stepped aside as the stretcher was lifted by willing hands and carried back along the jetty to the waiting helicopter.

Gemma watched the tall figure walking beside it, his back broad and strong, his dark hair glinting in the bright morning sunlight.

He didn't say goodbye, she thought sadly, then turned to bid Sam farewell.

'I'll run you back to your car,' a voice called, and she looked up to see Grant waiting on the wharf. She looked at her watch, surprised to see that it was only half-past seven, and that the day still stretched ahead with all it usual problems.

'Thanks, Grant,' she said gratefully, clambering up to stand beside him on the old timbers as the rotor of the helicopter started whirling and the noise of the engine precluded further conversation.

Grant's arm came round her, and, as Sam had earlier, he held her close, dropping a light kiss on the top of her head, then walked, his arm still around her shoulders, back down the long jetty.

The noise intensified and the helicopter lifted, and Gemma raised her head and followed it with her eyes until it whirled over the hills behind the town and disappeared from view.

'You OK?' Grant asked, and she nodded.

'I'll go out again now,' she said firmly, knowing that, at last, the time for mourning her father was over, and a new chapter in her life was beginning.

The waiting-room was already crowded when she arrived for work—late! She'd rung the hospital from home, then had two house-calls that could not be put off.

'I'm sorry,' she said to the room at large as she hurried through, but the smiles that followed her were concerned and understanding. The town would already know about this morning's accident!

Janey Carr was the first patient, a contemporary of Vicky's though more worldly-wise at fifteen than Vicki would ever be.

'I'm not sick and I don't need an examination but I want some tablets to help me lose weight,' she said bluntly, and Gemma sighed.

Looking down at Janey's file, she noted the weight, height and blood-pressure readings her nurse had taken while the girl waited.

'You're not overweight, Janey,' she said carefully. Her eyes told her it was unlikely to be pregnancy, but she'd have to check if she could, without alienating the already defensive child-woman. 'It's natural, at your age, for the weight to shift around a bit so that you end up with more on your hips and buttocks. It's what makes you different from the boys!'

'I've put on five kilograms in the last six months,' the girl replied, her lips set in a mutinous line. 'I don't care what my weight should be; I know I'm fat.'

'Well,' Gemma said carefully, her mind recalling Vicky's desire to be on the Pill, 'five kilograms in six months is a lot. The best thing to do is to see what might have caused it. Have you started buying lunch at school, had a sudden craze for chocolate milk shakes, stopped walking to the bus stop? Usually there's a reason for sudden weight gain.'

The girl looked interested, and stopped being resentful for long enough to think back, but finally she shook her head.

'I do eat sensibly,' she said. 'I know all about anorexia and things. I don't want to be like that!'

'That's great,' Gemma assured her, then added as casually as she could, 'But if it's not a change in your diet, it has be to something else. What about your periods? Are they regular?' The girl nodded, and mentioned when she'd had her last one, too secure and confident for Gemma to believe otherwise. She pursued her other option! 'Are you on a contraceptive pill for any reason?'

Seeing the colour fluctuate in the girl's cheeks, she knew she had hit the truth.

Janey nodded, and Gemma continued as calmly as she could, 'Well, maybe we could look at what you're taking. Some people put on weight while others don't. And sometimes it happens for the first few months while your body adjusts. If you'd like to try another type, we could do that, but, in the meantime, it's school holidays and there's no excuse for not getting a bit of extra exercise. You're a keen board rider, aren't you?'

Again her patient nodded, glad to have skipped over the dangerous ground as lightly as they had. 'I haven't done much lately,' she admitted. 'I broke up with my boyfriend and don't want to surf in that group any more.'

Because his new girl is in it, I assume, Gemma thought, again feeling the helplessness of an adult to protect adolescents from the pain of growing up.

'Surf with the girls for a while,' she suggested. 'Get out there on the waves and forget the boys; they'll soon come back to join you if they see you're having fun without them! Keep busy and keep moving, get plenty of exercise, and if you don't start to lose a bit of weight, and are still worried about it, come back and see me. Better still, come back and see me anyway!'

'Thanks!' the girl said cheerfully, and left the room, unaware of the tension and anger that her short visit had triggered in the local doctor.

Throughout the morning, she worked with part of her mind teasing at what seemed an insoluble problem.

Mary Parsons, freed from the responsibility of the shop with the excuse of the visiting grandchildren, was in for her regular check-up.

'The baby's taking that awful mixture from the bottle now,' she reported.

'I'm glad,' Gemma replied, then gave her the results of her latest blood tests. 'Now, with that good news we can step up the exercise. What about dancing? You and Dave used to be the stars at the Saturday night hops if I remember rightly. It's great aerobic exercise if you can persuade him to join you. The bowling club has started regular Tuesday night fifty-fifty sessions.'

'We've thought about going, but haven't got round to it yet,' Mary admitted. 'Actually,' she confided, 'Dave's been after me to go, but until I started the diet and the walks I had no energy for anything.'

'Well, get yourself off there now,' Gemma told her as she walked with her to the door. 'You'll be doing your body a favour and putting a bit of fun back into your lives.'

The morning stretched into afternoon. A sandwich and a glass of milk, eaten at her desk, provided enough sustenance to keep going, but through all the different complaints and symptoms, the concerns that Janey's visit had provoked remained niggling in the back of Gemma's mind.

'I think it's a spider bite of some kind, but I've never reacted this way before.' Mrs Warren was in her late sixties, a keen gardener who invariably brought a cutting of some rare plant for Gemma when she visited.

Now she lifted her drill skirt and revealed a round, angry red mark on her inner thigh.

'Is it painful?' Gemma asked, but received a negative shake of the head.

'Not there,' Mrs Warren told her, 'but my leg and hip have been playing up. Not like rheumatism, but painful, like a pinched nerve.'

Using a light and magnifying glasses, Gemma examined the disturbance, noting the raised spots and, in the centre, a few water-filled blebs.

'Slip off your skirt and let me see your back,' she requested, guessing, but hoping she was wrong.

Mrs Warren turned around, and Gemma saw the line of spots, irregularly scattered along the sciatic nerve, from where it left the spinal cord, across one buttock, and down on to the thigh.

'It's shingles, I'm afraid,' she said, handing the elderly patient her skirt, and watching as she pulled it back on and fastened it. 'There's a new drug out that's extraordinarily effective, but shingles can still be unpleasant, and have lingering after-effects, so I want you to take it easy.' She smiled, and added, 'Like staying out of that garden for a few days.'

Pulling a prescription pad and drug guide towards her, she explained as she wrote.

'It's a disease related to chickenpox——'

'Have I caught it from the kids around the place? Everyone seems to have it!'

'No, it's a funny thing,' Gemma told her, 'but, while someone with shingles could pass chickenpox to a child, it's rare the other way round. Must be pure coincidence! It usually means you've had a mild dose of chickenpox yourself as a child, and the virus lies dormant in the spine until it's triggered—often by stress?'

She looked enquiringly across the table.

'I don't get stressed,' her patient said firmly. 'I'm an old-fashioned person and that's a new-fangled disease.'

'Have you got the family home for Christmas?' Gemma probed, and received an answering nod.

'Then that could have been enough, especially as you were a bit run down after that bout of flu in October.'

'This might be an excuse to take to my bed and ignore the lot of them,' Mrs Warren suggested with a wry grin.

'Still fighting with each other, those girls of yours?'

'They never stop!' the other woman agreed wearily. 'See each other once a year and take up where they left off last time. I don't know why they come. Their husbands must hate it! Spoilt 'em both, I did, encouraging them to have careers! If they'd had a bunch of kids, they might behave better!'

Gemma looked up, and saw the sadness in the dark eyes.

'Tell them you're to go to bed and stay there,' she advised cheerfully. 'Let them do the shopping and cooking, and look after you for a change.'

She pushed the finished scripts across the desk.

'These, Zovirax, are a compound called acyclovir, which is a relatively new discovery and should prevent a worse dose, and help you over them more quickly. You have to take ten a day for seven days.'

Mrs Warren nodded, and Gemma continued. 'The prednisone is a corticosteroid which, hopefully, will help prevent the neuralgia-like pain that usually follows shingles and can affect you for months afterwards. You take two a day for two days, then one and a half for two days, then one, and so on. It's written down here, and by next week you'll be breaking them in quarters. It's important with any corticosteroids to ease off the dosage, and not stop taking them abruptly.'

Again she shuffled papers, and pointed again. 'This is an antipruritic; it'll stop the itching and discomfort, but could make you drowsy. Take one each morning and evening until the itchiness goes. This cream, Stoxil, will help allay the irritation,' she added, pointing to the last scribble on the sheets, 'but it's such a little tube it won't go far!'

'I'll be rattling,' Mrs Warren joked as she gathered up the prescription forms.

'The Zovirax is the most important,' Gemma warned. 'And the prednisone! The others you can do without, but those should help you through it and minimise the after-effects. And in the meantime,' she added with a smile, 'even if you don't feel sick, play the invalid!'

'I might just do that,' came the quick reply. 'Maybe those girls need a little shock treatment!'

Gemma watched her depart, thinking how hard it must be for doctors who bought into or set up a practice in an unfamiliar town. Often, a background knowledge of the person helped both diagnosis and possible treatment. A new doctor would learn, if he or she took the time, and had sufficient interest and enthusiasm, but a local would always have a slight edge.

The thought brought her back to Janey, and Vicky. All the teenagers in town went into Craigstown by bus to high school. Were the girls seeing a doctor in town for their prescriptions for contraceptives? And was this doctor counselling them at the same time, and watching for possible side-effects?

'Craigstown Hospital on the line for you,' Karen told her as she lifted the receiver to halt the muted buzzing noise.

'It's Sister Allen, Dr Wainwright,' a firm voice said, and Gemma tried, but failed, to place the speaker. 'Dr Griffiths asked me to phone you to say they took the young man into Theatre and he thinks they've saved the leg.'

'Oh, that is good news,' Gemma replied happily, and she felt a physical easing of tension throughout her body. 'Thank you so much for letting me know. I'll pass on the news to his friends here.'

She hung up with a smile that faded a little when she wondered why Simon had not rung himself.

'Don't be ridiculous,' she muttered, shaking her head frustratedly as she accepted her own contrariness. 'You don't want the man chasing after you all through the summer holidays, yet you're disppointed that he hasn't rung. Get real, Gemma!'

'Talking to yourself is one bad sign,' Karen said as she slid through the door with another pile of files. 'You're down to the last three patients but Michael Dodds has brought in that little boy who has cerebral palsy. He was playing cricket with a tennis racket and somehow used his head for a ball. Blood everywhere, of course, as the cut's right above his eyes, but a couple of stitches should fix it. Will you see him next?'

'I'd better,' Gemma told her, 'but please apologise to the other patients for me. I haven't been able to catch up all day!'

Four stitches sealed the wound, and she prescribed an antibiotic to ward off possible infection, first checking the records Michael had brought with him for possible allergies. As she chatted to Michael about Maggie, and the progress of the chickenpox, she felt the effects of the long day beginning to creep up on her.

Three to go! she thought as they disappeared through the door, and she opened the next file.

By the time she was finished, the room had darkened. Karen rang through to say goodbye, with a stern order for Gemma to go home immediately! Ignoring her friend's concern, she wrote up notes and dictated two letters to specialists into the little dictaphone she kept on her desk, before finally pushing back her chair and thinking about leaving.

The problem that had nagged in her subconscious all day raised itself again and she felt a kind of anger stirring. Was the person prescribing the contraceptives behaving responsibly?

'Don't you know that doctor's surgeries are targeted by thieves? You're supposed to lock up when everyone goes!'

Simon's deep voice frightened her so much that she leapt out of her chair, her heart thudding uncomfortably.

'Everyone's not gone,' she said weakly. 'I'm still here.'

'That only makes it worse!' he said severely, a suggestion of anger bristling in his voice. 'I could have been a crazed drug addict, willing to kill to get what I want.'

'I'm glad you weren't,' she said, smiling slightly at the picture he'd conjured up. 'I wouldn't have had the strength to resist!'

'Oh, is that a fact? I'll take that as encouragement!' he murmured, switching back to the casual charmer. Gemma blushed when she realised the connotation he had put on the words.

'What are you doing here?' she asked, anxious to change the subject. 'I did get your message, by the way. I was pleased to hear about that boy's leg. Did they let you help? Will he be OK?'

'Whoa there!' he said with a lazy kind of grin that made her insides melt. 'One question at a time, and not here, I think. How about we go over to the Fish Kettle and see what Grant has to tempt our jaded appetites?'

'Your appetite might be jaded, but I don't eat out often enough for mine to be anything other than voracious!' How easy it was to laugh with this man, she thought as she smiled up at him and waited for his response.

'I can almost read those big eyes of yours,' he murmured, his gaze catching and holding hers. 'Almost, but not quite!'

His swift metamorphosis from teasing friend and colleague to romantic pursuer threw her into confusion again, and she knew it would be obvious in her burning cheeks.

'I can't keep eating with you!' she protested.

'Because people will talk?'

'Partly that,' she admitted, 'but also because. . .' She couldn't explain; she didn't know herself why not, just that it was wrong somehow—and dangerous. And very, very tempting!

CHAPTER SIX

'TELL me about the boy's leg?'

They were sitting on the edge of the jetty, their legs dangling over the dark, oily-looking water. Beyond them were the masts and spars of the fishing boats—*Frantic Fan*, *The Jane* and *Two Bits*—and, beyond these squat trawlers, the shorter jetty with more of the fleet tied up.

They must be fishing the early morning tides at the moment. The thought eased into Gemma's mind, an innate knowledge it seemed she'd been born with! The men who worked the boats would sleep until midnight, then make their way down here and motor out beyond the heads, to find the delicacies the tourists and the southern markets wanted.

The smell of fish and diesel and the low gurgle and slap of the turning tide against the hulls imprinted the time and place on her senses, storing them as memories for later years.

After pleading that she was too tired and too grubby to go anywhere for dinner, Gemma had allowed herself to be persuaded into fish and chips, which they had eaten with enthusiasm, straight from the paper, here on the deserted jetty above the river. Gemma rolled the paper into a ball and stuffed it into her oversize shoulder-bag while she waited for Simon to speak.

'His name's Gavin Wells, and he's up from Sydney for the holidays. His family knows Sam's, it seems,' Simon began, bringing Gemma's drifting mind back to the present. 'He was lucky!' he added almost under his breath, then continued with his story. 'There's a chap in Craigstown who's fanatical about microsurgery, which means the gear in the new theatre at the hospital is as good as in any big city theatre. He was also on hand, having been called in for the accident victims.'

'John Sinclair, was it?' Gemma asked, her voice relaxed as she enjoyed the quiet communion with nature in the company of a colleague. 'I've not met him but keep hearing about his work.'

'He's good,' Simon assured her. 'He patched up the blood vessels first then checked along nerve fibres as fine as silk thread for breaks or damage before I got a look in!'

'There was no other orthopod disputing your claim?' Gemma teased. They were perhaps a foot apart, but she could feel his presence like a physical warmth, secure and comforting—like sitting in front of a fire, she thought dreamily, then remembered the conversation. 'No one who said, Go away, stranger!'

'Would they dare?' he mocked, one eyebrow rising with quizzical good humour. 'Actually, I found out that there were two specialists in town until recently, when one packed up to return to the bright city lights. The chap who stayed is on holidays at the moment and the micro-man is covering for him. Once he'd done all the delicate bits, he was happy for me to do the heavy work!'

Gemma listened in silence, following the procedure in her mind. 'But how can you immobilise the bone into a position where it will heal cleanly, with all the flesh and tissue damage?'

'Little ignoramus!' he chided. 'Did you forget all your orthopaedic studies the minute you opted for the easy life of a small-town GP.'

'Easy life! That'd be the day,' she retorted, but did not argue further as he started to explain.

'I stabilised the bone with skeletal pins and wires—ordinary open reduction technique——'

'Very ordinary!' Gemma muttered, but he ignored the taunt.

'—then attached them to external fixators. That way, the wound is accessible for observation and dressings, but the lad's got support for the bone when we get him on his feet.'

'Which should be as soon as possible, I suppose,' Gemma added doubtfully, thinking of the messy wound and the dangers of a deep vein thrombosis or fatty embolism, both of which were potentially fatal complications.

'Yes! Although he's young, he's got all three of the triad of factors that could produce an intravascular thrombosis—with the extra blood products, stasis of blood flow and damage to the vessel walls—so the sooner we get him mobile the better.'

Gemma sensed a deep satisfaction behind the professional calm and was both surprised and pleased by it. This man had not become blasé about the specialised knowledge and skills he possessed. She sighed with an inexplicable pleasure and settled her shoulders more comfortably against the bollard behind them.

'How did you leave him?' she asked, wanting to keep him talking while she sat back and enjoyed the deep cadence of his voice.

'Most uncomfortable, I should imagine.' Simon chuckled. 'He's hitched up to an overhead trapeze, he's got drainage tubes coming from deep in the wound, a catheter, a drip still in his arm, and this weird metal frame protruding all around his lower leg. Not to mention the fact that he's probably in considerable pain!'

'At least he's still got a lower leg,' Gemma told him.

'Who knows what might have happened if you hadn't been on hand?'

'He could still lose it, Gemma,' he said seriously. 'The risk of infection is increased when we have to pin the bone. Despite all the sterile procedures, we are still introducing something foreign into the bone's medullary canal, and we can also cause further tissue damage with the devices themselves.'

'You've done all you can,' Gemma assured him, hearing the doubts in his deep voice and feeling a strong tug of empathy.

They sat on in silence, while the night air wrapped around them like a blanket, and the soothing sounds of the water relaxed their minds and bodies.

'How's your day been?' Simon broke the silence with the quietly spoken question.

'Please retract that question; my day is better not mentioned!' Gemma said quickly, not wanting to think about her own work or its attendant problems.

'Trouble, or just too much work?'

The sympathy in the man's voice was seductive, but she couldn't burden him with her problems. She sighed again but remained silent.

'You'll feel better when you've talked about it,' he told her, tempting her confession with an unspoken promise of understanding.

'I probably won't,' she retaliated as she gave in to the temptation. Bitterness crept into her voice as the frustration she had felt on and off all day flickered back to life. 'I'm more likely to get angry and end up yelling, and that won't achieve anything!'

'Do you often get angry and end up yelling?' There was a lazy interest in the question!

'No—well—not all that often!'

'That's good,' he told her, moving slightly so that his

shirt-sleeve brushed tantalisingly against her bare arm, 'although a little bit of fire adds spice to a relationship.'

'Speaking from personal experience, no doubt!' she said smartly. 'Not that there's any "relationship" between us to add spice to.'

'Isn't there?'

She knew he had turned his head and was looking at her, but she stared resolutely out over the dark water. If she turned to look at him, his lips would be too close, and his eyes might see the regret that had stabbed her as she spoke.

'No,' she snapped, then added positively, 'And nor is there likely to be.'

'Friendship's the basis of any relationship,' he argued. 'We're friends, aren't we?'

'Acquaintances,' she corrected him, trying to dampen the insidious intimacy he had insinuated into the conversation.

'Well, tell an acquaintance your problems—apart from the usual over-work, and holiday population explosion aggravations.' He spoke with a natural authority, his voice slow and deep, and as he finished he reached out and took her hand, clasping it in his strong, warming paw with a comforting assurance.

There was nothing flirtatious in the gesture, yet Gemma felt her fingers responding to his grip, answering his touch with a slight, affirmative pressure. She thought for a few moments, choosing her words carefully, aware how easily her disgruntled feelings could be misinterpreted as 'sour grapes'.

'I think some of the young girls from here are seeing someone in Craigstown for contraceptive pills,' she said baldly, trying to pull her hand away as she realised that talking about the problem was making her angry again and the anger would project towards her audience of one.

He held on tightly, his thumb stroking the back of her fingers with the lightest of touches, but he did not speak.

'I'm not making a moral judgement about this,' she went on defensively. 'I wouldn't do that! No one has the right to do that for someone else. I've prescribed it myself to young girls. What worries me is that I can't be certain that whoever they are seeing is actually doing the right thing by them.'

'Aren't you showing a great lack of trust in your fellow practitioners?' His voice was bland, deliberately neutral, yet it fired her up more than a specific criticism would have done.

'Yes, I am, and with reason!' she stormed. 'These kids get to know who'll prescribe contraceptives with no questions asked, and word gets round. It's probably the same old fellow who was in town when I was at school there. We all knew you went to him, told him you had bad period pains and, bingo, there was your script.'

'Is that so bad?' Was he interested, or simply testing to see if she *was* guilty of the moral judgement she had denied earlier?

'It is if they're only thirteen and still growing. The effects of oestrogen on growth haven't been fully documented, but there's enough evidence to make one recommend something else if at all possible.'

'But even elderly medicos would be aware of that,' he protested, while his thumb continued to soothe her with its rhythmic motion on her fingers.

'Yes, but they're not aware of the ages of some of these kids,' she explained. 'If a girl comes in who looks sixteen, and tells you she's sixteen, what do you do? You believe her. She's quite likely to be twelve and a half, but we can't ask for birth certificates and ID from patients.'

'If she looks sixteen, she's probably finished growing,' he argued, obviously enjoying his role as devil's advocate.

'But hardly maturing!' Gemma said harshly. 'And that's another thing that worries me. Do the girls' parents know? Should they know? If the girl's a minor, who's responsible? And it's not only all that ethical side of things.'

'No?'

'No, Simon,' she said seriously. 'What do these girls know about the attendant risks of promiscuity? Is the doctor impressing on these kids that being on the Pill is not the answer to all the problems of adolescence? Is he or she cautioning them about safe sex? Are they getting regular physical checks to ensure that the hormones they are taking are not having adverse side-effects that the kids themselves are unaware can even happen?'

'All these questions and no answers!' he murmured as a breeze sprang up and lifted tendrils of hair that had escaped their confining braid, easing the damp strands from off her hot face. 'You have had a bad day!'

He tugged on the hand he still held, and somehow drew her closer, until she rested partly on the solid timber post and partly against his firm shoulder.

Lacking the strength or the will to push away, she lay there, savouring the clean, male scent of him, mingled with the familiar aromas of the harbour.

'You can't watch over all your patients all the time, Gemma,' he said quietly, his lips moving against her hair with an insidious softness. 'Nor can you give them more than what they want from you. You're a doctor, not some omnipotent presence!'

'I know all that,' she mumbled, vaguely ashamed of

her outburst, 'but I can't help worrying. Can't help wishing there was something I could do!'

'Don't we all?' he responded cheerfully, tightening his arm around her shoulders and giving her a comforting squeeze. 'You think I'm holding you like this to offer a little comfort—one colleague to another, of course—but actually I'm clinging to you the way a drowning man clings to a bit of flotsam, to try and stop myself rushing into Craigstown to see how my own patient is.'

While the ready hint of humour was audible in his voice, there was a serious undertone, and Gemma pulled away from him so that she could look at his face.

A slight, shamefaced grin met her eyes in the dusky twilight, and he nodded as if to confirm what he had said. Then he bent his head and his lips met hers with a gentle certainty.

They were warm, and firm, and dry, and they pressed against hers as if to learn the contours of her flesh through their touch; as if to leave their mark, indelibly imprinted on her nerve-endings. Was it for a minute or an hour that they sat, their bodies motionless as their lips told each other secrets for which there were no words?

Her breathing quickened and her lips parted as she tried to drag more air into her lungs. It was a mistake! In that instant, she felt the sweet invasive moistness of his tongue, gently probing, teasing and withdrawing, leaving a taste that was uniquely him, a taste she wanted to savour, and remember.

A helplessness overwhelmed her, separating her mind from her body. She seemed to float above their searching lips, feeling the melting, drowning sensations that invaded her body with a clinical detachment.

It ended, as kisses must, and she felt a sense of loss

as they moved apart and sat in silence, looking out into the growing darkness. Her body tingled with an increasing awareness of his, her lips felt tender—acutely sensitised by his touch—and her senses yearned for something more.

'I think we kiss OK, don't you?' he said finally, calm detachment in the words. For all the world like a scientist discussing the results of an experiment, Gemma decided, and felt the fleeting sadness of regret.

Not knowing what to say, she ignored him, but she was beginning to discover that such behaviour had no effect on him whatsoever. He simply pursued his point in his own time and his own way.

Out to the east, the lightening sky signalled the rising moon, and the night noises seemed to intensify as they sat in silence. Gemma shifted slightly, feeling the hardness of the old timbers beneath her as her body ached for a comfort her mind would not acknowledge.

'Shall we have a nice light-hearted affair?' he asked at last, putting no more emphasis on the words than if he'd asked if she wanted a cup of coffee after dinner.

'I don't think so,' she said carefully, hoping that she had achieved the right degree of casualness in her own voice. Would he guess how confused she felt? Could he feel her body's strong attraction towards him, throbbing across the space that separated them like radio waves moving unseen through the air?

'I think we'd both enjoy it,' he went on, as carelessly as if he were still discussing after-dinner coffee.

'No doubt,' Gemma responded crossly, unable to play his game any longer, 'but as there's absolutely no future in it, why bother? While it might be a nice little Christmas diversion for you, I'm the one who's working all hours of the day and night, and, if we did have an affair, I'd be missing out on even more sleep in order to satisfy your sexual urges while you're on holidays.'

'Do you not have sexual urges?' he asked in the same expressionless tone, infuriating Gemma even more.

'Of course I do!' she stormed. 'But I don't go picking up strange holiday-makers who stray into my surgery to assuage them!'

'Being that you're the local doctor with a big reputation to uphold!' he taunted, as if that would explain her reluctance to indulge in casual affairs.

'It's got nothing to do with my reputation!' The words snapped out and she clenched her fists into tight balls, trying to quell a desperate urge to thump the man. 'Although I think the people here might be disappointed in me if I carried on with a different tourist each week!'

The thought diverted her for an instant as she saw a vivid picture of a trail of discarded lovers, men of all shapes and sizes, leaving the surgery! She almost smiled, then realised she must be serious if she wanted to get her feelings across to this infuriating man.

'It's because normal people don't behave that way. Well, I don't anyway,' she added, afraid that he might condemn her for the sweeping generalisation. 'There's more to life than a bit of casual sex, you know!'

She paused, then shook her head, unable to believe all the things she'd been goaded into thinking and even saying.

'This is a ridiculous conversation,' she told him, swinging her legs around on to the jetty and standing up carefully. 'I have neither the time nor the inclination to have an affair with you, and I see no reason why I should have to justify that decision.'

He remained sitting where he was, but looked up at her, his dark face half lit by the rising moon. She could see his profile, strong and clean, and the quick flicker of an eyelid as he actually winked at her.

'Still friends?' Two soft, seductive words that coiled their way into her heart!

Once again she felt the air leave her lungs as if expelled by giant bellows.

'I suppose so,' she muttered ungraciously. 'Although if I had any sense at all I'd push you into the water here and now and hope you'd drown! I've a feeling I'd be doing myself a favour!'

She turned away and stumped back along the echoing boards. Her mind repeated the things she had said, as if to strengthen her decision, but the whisper in her heart had not been spoken! The reason she was resisting this man's perverse attraction was not simply a distaste for transient affairs, but the certainty that it would not be enough, and that she would be left, alone and hurting, at the end of it!

She hugged her arms around herself, as if to comfort a body not yet in distress. Behind her, a boat creaked against its mooring, and the sound brought back memories of her childhood. Think back, not forward, she told herself, seeking the security of a youth free of responsibility and moral dilemmas.

She stood very still and listened, lifting her head to sniff the air. With a sense of wonder, she realised that the sadness had gone from the past, and in its place was a piercing sweetness that flooded her being, and lightened her step as she turned and walked back determinedly towards the trawlers.

'Coming back to tell me you've changed your mind?' He was on his feet, but still—leaning against the bollard now—totally relaxed as he took in the peaceful beauty of the night.

'Coming back to look at the boats,' she corrected him, then felt ridiculously pleased when he moved towards her.

'Just look?'

'Well. . .no! I'm going to climb down and walk around on the *Fan*.'

'Re-live the drama of the morning?' he queried.

'No,' she replied, her heart full of trepidation. 'Just bury a ghost!' He said nothing, and she felt obliged to add, 'I won't be long, but if you want to go I'll walk home. It's not far and the exercise won't hurt me.'

He did not reply, but nor did he go. Instead, he fell into step beside her, his footsteps beating a bass rhythm to her lighter ones, the sounds strangely synchronised. She found the echoing beat, and his nearness, reassuring. They reached the end of the jetty and she swung down on to the deck of the trawler.

He did not follow her, but she could see the dark shape of him above her on the jetty as she moved lightly round the boat, touching the nets, the old timber of the spars, the fraying rope that edged the railings. She repeated the familiar names to herself like a litany.

Frantic Fan—the boat named after her mother—the effervescent Elvis Presley fan who had been holidaying here at Grange Bay when her father met, wooed and won her. Not for them the ordinary naming—*The Lucy* it could have been—but something different—something that had a special meaning for the two of them.

Memories flooded back—old stories of her parents' courtship, her mother's decision to stay on when her holiday had ended—'just in case there might be something in it', she'd once told Gemma.

Her parents' love for each other had been like a beacon, strong and steadfast throughout her childhood, yet her mother had made a new life for herself—had found a new love—while Gemma had remained trapped in the past!

She stood on the deck beneath the mainmast for a

minute, seeing the crossbeams and spars, the net rigging and crane jib, black against the velvety purple of the sky. Then she turned to leave, her silent farewell sent out into the star-filled magic of the night.

Clambering back on to the railings to hitch herself up on to the jetty, she felt Simon's hands grasp her arms and he reached down and pulled her up as easily as if she were a child. His strong arms came around her as she steadied herself, and he held her close for a long moment.

'My father died after an accident on that boat, ten years ago,' she said. Her voice was low and even, muffled against his shirt. 'I'd finished high school and was on holidays—the last before leaving Grange Bay to go to university in Sydney. It was a magic summer—totally carefree—with all the hard work of those final years behind me.'

The memory was so clear she could feel the irresponsible delight of those days race through her body, and longed, for an instant, to recapture that little bit of her youth.

'I was out with them that night. I went out often—always had done. The light on the masthead wasn't working and he climbed up, as he'd done a thousand times before.'

His arms did not tighten, and he did not move, but she felt his sympathy as the words fell from her lips of their own volition, coming out in a rush like the water streaming from the nets as they were hauled into the trawlers.

'The boat pitched unexpectedly and he fell. It was a stupid accident, over so quickly it couldn't possibly have been serious! But he didn't get up!'

She spoke the words as carefully and unemotionally as a narrator in a film, but now his arms did gather her closer, and his hands moved against her back in an age-old motion of comfort.

'There was very little blood. I actually felt the ridged edges that I learnt about years later. "You'll feel the edges of a depressed skull fracture," the lecturer said. "Feel lightly, don't go poking and probing!" The memory stayed in my fingers, not my mind!'

She paused, then breathed in deeply.

'The crew radioed ahead for an ambulance and brought the boat in. The only doctor in town had retired and gone to live in Queensland. All that the ambulance men could do was take him straight to town. He died on the way to hospital.'

Simon remained silent, as if some sixth sense had told him she had to tell the story in her own way and in her own time, to say the words that had been bottled up for too long.

'Later, I realised that there must have been massive brain damage, with the swelling causing downward herniation and cutting off the vascular supply through the brain stem. At the time, I knew, somehow, that he was sinking deeper into unconsciousness, and the helplessness is very hard to forget.'

'Could a doctor have saved him?' Simon asked the question she had asked herself a million times.

'I honestly don't know. All I can go on are my feelings. If a doctor had been there, I would have felt we'd done all we could. I know that's irrational, Simon. I know the medical facts, but somehow it makes no difference to how I feel.'

'It's why you came back here?'

She nodded against his chest.

'It wasn't that I was expected to. . .' She tried to explain. 'Although the people here raised money to help me go away to university. But all through the course, when specialities begin to tempt other students,

I knew I wanted to be a GP. To me, that's what medicine was about, the reason I was doing it. If a doctor had set up a practice in Grange Bay any time in those intervening years, I'd have been pleased, and gone somewhere else when I finished.'

'But no one did and you felt you had to come back.'

Now she shook her head, denying pressure or coercion.

'I wanted to come back!' she told him honestly. 'I realised that I'd been hoping no one would come, and the day I did come back was one of the happiest days of my life.'

'And the town welcomed you back with open arms?'

She paused, thinking back to the very mixed reaction she had received.

'Not exactly!' she admitted. 'All the men would have preferred a male doctor and most of the older people, male and female, would have much preferred a stranger.'

'Hard for them to believe the child they had known could be so wise?' he murmured.

'What beginner in any profession is wise?' she demanded, rejecting his sympathy and understanding as they weakened her resolve and sneaked under her defences. 'I felt annoyed at first—especially as I could have starved to death, with so many of them continuing to make the trek to Craigstown to see their regular GP. I'm certain even those who did switch to me went back to their former doctors to have my diagnosis or treatment confirmed!'

He gave a great shout of laughter that echoed through her body with a sweet joy.

'And have you won them over now?'

'Most of them,' she admitted, 'although many of the older men still travel to town. I don't blame them. It can take years to get used to a new doctor so why bother when you have a perfectly good one?'

'But it's now a viable practice and you could sell out if you wanted to move?'

'If viability is based on hours worked and money made, it would be extremely attractive for someone buying in, but. . .' She moved now, pushing away from him and studying him intently as she continued. 'I think I must be a small-town person,' she confessed earnestly. 'I love my lifestyle here, in spite of the Christmas horrors. I love the town and the people. I belong here.'

Although she spoke the words to the man who stood beside her in the moonlight, they were also a re-affirmation of her decision to return to Grange Bay, and they brought her a sense of ease and inner peace.

'It would have been easier to practise in a town where you knew no one, where you didn't feel personally responsible.'

She nodded. 'That's what I used to think, but I know the responsibility is part of the job, and learning to cope with it is part of learning to be a good doctor.'

'And are you a good doctor, sweet Alice?' he asked, laughter lurking again behind the words.

'Not yet,' she admitted after seriously considering his question, 'but I will be one day. One day, when I have learned to stand aside and be dispassionate, when I've learned to let some problems alone for time to solve, not worry them to death like a dog with a rag between its teeth.'

He reached out and held her close again.

'Do you want to know my prescripton?' he whispered, his lips in her hair once again.

'Probably not,' she muttered gruffly, disturbed by the fire his body ignited within hers. 'But no doubt you'll tell me anyway.'

But he did not speak.

She felt him stir, then his lips touched the skin on her forehead, as if in farewell. It was a light, feathery touch that made her want to shiver, yet something inside her ached for more, and she raised her head and pressed against him, her body sending its own messages, her lips seeking his.

It was a kiss that made her wonder if she'd ever been kissed before. She felt the sensations it aroused trickling down her spine, and tingling in her toes. Her blood seemed to bubble in her veins as it raced around her body, firing nerve-endings she did not know she had, and melting her tissues into a molten heat.

Her lips trembled against his, and her body pressed closer, seeking a support that only he could give. It seemed to her that they were joined, the air they breathed shared between them, so that she could feel his feelings in it, and hear his thoughts.

His hands moved against her spine, kneading her flesh with a tender power. Then, with fingers splayed against her shoulder-blades, he pressed her closer against his cheek. Her breasts throbbed, pulsing with the rapid beating of her heart, and aching with their own arousal.

Her own hands moved without restraint, feeling the warmth of his body beneath his cotton shirt, the flat slabs of muscle over the hard boniness of his ribs. They slid up his neck, rubbing against the prickly, short-clipped hair, then on into the softness. Her fingers curled around the strands and tightened on them as the hunger his kiss was awakening took control, and her body cried out for satisfaction.

'Shall we rethink the affair?' he asked, in such an undertone that she could barely hear the words, but rather read the meaning from his closeness.

Unable to trust herself to answer, she clung to him,

then felt him move away, his hands on her shoulders, steadying her.

'Tomorrow!' he added, as if the word should make perfect sense to her.

'Tomorrow?' she repeated stupidly, forcing an exceedingly foggy brain to work.

She looked up to see him watching her, his face shadowed, but his eyes gleaming with secret messages she could no longer read. She shook her head as if to clear it, or deny what he was doing to her, and he grinned sympathetically and slid an arm around her shoulders, leading her back towards the car.

'Time you were home in bed,' he told her, then must have felt her tremble, for he dropped a kiss on her head and said one more word; 'Alone!'

Settling back into the comfortable leather seats in the big vehicle, Gemma felt the draining tiredness that the pleasure of Simon's company had held at bay creeping into her body. She remained silent while he drove her home, then helped her out of the car.

A momentary flutter of fear, or excitement, shimmered through her as he walked her to her front door. If he kissed her again, would she still be able to say no? She was too tired to make decisions!

'You can give me an answer tomorrow,' he said calmly as she unlocked the door, and he turned to leave. 'One should never make decisions at night!'

CHAPTER SEVEN

GEMMA saw the Range Rover as soon as she turned on to the esplanade, and, as something skipped lightly inside her, she had to fight down a contrary impulse to turn around and drive back home. Self-preservation told her to run, while every cell in her body seemed to tingle with a weird anticipatory delight.

'How're things?' Grant had come to greet her as she walked from her car and now fell in beside her as she led the way down on to the sand.

'Fine, Grant,' she replied absent-mindly as she wondered why she'd hurried past Simon, talking to Bob about yesterday's accident, with no more than a polite, unsmiling nod.

Would he come up and walk with her, or catch up with her when they reached the track? Would he want an answer to his ridiculous suggestion? Was it so ridiculous? Her mind argued back and forth, achieving nothing but confusion.

'Are you listening, Gemma?' Grant was saying in the exasperated way he had spoken to her all her life.

'I'm sorry, Grant!' She gave him a quick smile, and forced her jangled brain to concentrate on the present.

'I was wondering what you were doing on Christmas Day. I'll be working, of course, but I'd like you to be my guest for lunch at the restaurant. Dave and Mary and their family will be there. Bill's at home; you'd enjoy seeing him again.'

Would I? Gemma wondered. Or would the sight of all the happy families merely remind me of what I'm missing?

'I've already told Suzi and Michael I'll go out to Orana. They are officially on days off but there are a couple of kids whose families were going walking in the mountains over the holidays, and the Dodds agreed to keep their offspring for Christmas.'

'Well, if you want to come in for dinner when you get back, you'd be more than welcome,' Grant said stiffly, and Gemma wondered what she'd done to annoy him.

The morning was fresh and clear, and she forced herself to relax and take in the beauty of the new day. They climbed up past where the helicopter had landed only twenty-four hours earlier. With all that had happened since, it could have been a lifetime ago, Gemma thought, her mind wandering again from Grant's persistent conversation.

He was still behind her as they came on to the bush track, talking about people who'd been at school with them, and who were home for the holidays with their own families. Does Grant have this feeling of missing out on something as well? she wondered, striding briskly along the sandy path.

'I've got to check the diets,' she told him when the track widened and he moved up alongside. 'I assume, as you refuse to write out your list, that you're eating sensibly!'

He nodded and walked on, although she sensed a reluctance in him, as if all the words he'd spoken hadn't quite said what he'd wanted them to say!

'You're coping well, Mary, considering the time of the year,' Gemma assured the last of the dieters as they came down towards the town.

'I'm serious about this diet,' Mary confessed. 'I've hated being fat, and I can feel the difference in my energy level already.' She walked briskly on to join the others.

'I'm serious about something else,' the now familiar,

deep voice murmured in her ear as Simon moved up to take Mary's place by her side. Gemma felt a rush of heat firing her body into a tingling excitment. 'Like an answer to my question!' he added in a piercing undertone.

'I never make decisions before breakfast; you'll have to wait,' she teased. It was a mistake, she realised as she watched his face grow serious for a moment then a smile of great sweetness wrinkled his eyes and creased deep dimples into his cheeks.

'That's the first time you haven't said no,' he told her, his voice little more than a husky whisper.

A sudden hollowness overcame her, as if her vital organs had disintegrated into nothingness.

'I haven't said yes, either,' she warned him, warding off the weird faintness she felt with a strained laugh.

'I'll wait in hope,' he promised, and his stride lengthened as he led the way towards her car.

Grant was hovering beside it, and the men greeted each other with casual ease, then stood, one on either side of her, as if waiting for something to happen.

Now, why do I feel like a bone between two dogs? Gemma wondered.

'See you in the morning!' she said with a false brightness, unlocking the door and pulling it open.

'If you can't come Christmas Day, how about dinner tonight?' Grant asked, and Gemma felt a wave of dismay sweep over her. She looked down at the ground, determined not to look at Simon, who would, no doubt, be taking great delight in her confusion.

'I'll see what happens, Grant. Who knows what the day has in store for me? So far, the only predictable thing about these holidays has been their unpredictability. I'll call you, OK?'

He nodded, accepting her decision but obviously not liking it. Gemma felt a wrenching sympathy for him, thinking that, like her, he was unsettled by the season. He was an old friend, and she didn't want to hurt his feelings. 'I'll try to make it, I really will,' she assured him as she slipped into the car.

Simon Griffiths can make what he likes of that, she thought, but sharp barbs of disappointment prickled inside her as she drove off. She would far rather spend the evening with Simon, but he hadn't asked her! And then again, if she didn't intend having an affair with him, what was the point? Would he still want to see her? Probably not! Could she keep seeing him, and still say no? Again, probably not!

'Mrs Kelso rang and would like to see you this afternoon. Said she'd come at six unless you were busy. I said I'd ring her to confirm,' Karen greeted her when she arrived at the surgery, early for once. 'I felt like telling her you work hard enough as it is, without spoilt women piling their problems on you after work as well.'

Gemma looked at her in surprise, startled by the vehemence in Karen's usually placid voice.

'I think she's genuinely distressed, Karen,' she said mildly, but her friend would not be silenced.

'She's an unloader,' she said positively, handing Gemma a pile of files.

'An unloader?'

'Yes! The type who unloads all their problems on someone else, then goes off and enjoys life while the someone else worries.' Karen shut the filing-cabinet drawer with unnecessary force, punctuating her words with the sharp clang.

'Has she been unloading on you?' Gemma asked, wondering what had prompted this outburst.

'Only every time she rings,' Karen said with a sigh. 'I've been through separation and divorce, Gemma; I know how much it hurts. And I do feel sorry for her, but I get mad with myself when I keep falling for her tales of woe! I've even offered to mind the boys for her on Sunday, so she could spend the day with that dishy friend of hers.'

Stomachs not hearts are the true seat of the emotions, Gemma decided as she felt that organ twist with despair at the words.

'But there's nothing between them!' she blurted out. 'They're just old friends!'

'And who told you that, Madam Innocence?' Karen asked. 'Her or him?'

Apparently oblivious of the effect her words were having on her boss, Karen continued, 'Maybe there's nothing in it yet, but I'm certain Mrs Kelso has every intention of keeping the "friend" on a string until her husband either comes to heel, or decides to make the parting permenent.'

Patients began filtering into the room, and Gemma was glad to escape Karen's definitive reading of the situation and seek the sanctuary of her office. Her mind plunged into a welter of confusion, one part denying Karen's assumptions, another glad that gossip about herself and Simon was not yet spreading around town, and another tiny fragment desperately unhappy, although why she could not have said!

Fridays had become the day for monitoring the progress of pregnant patients. It had begun when she'd made appointments to check on those close to full term before the weekend. If the parents-to-be had opted for a homebirth, she could make sure that either the midwife or herself would be available.

Over her first twelve months, she had gradually discovered that the women enjoyed seeing each other while they waited, and an informal support network had developed. Now her other patients made appointments earlier in the week, leaving Friday free for maternity cases. Even those who were seeing an obstetrician in town and going there to have their babies came to Gemma on Fridays for their blood-pressure and urine checks.

Usually, it was a happy day, as she enjoyed the women's talk and the opportunity to be seeing well people rather than sick ones. Today, however, something was missing. The healthy bloom on the cheeks of her patients, the shy pride in their eyes, the stretching skin over their swollen bellies aggravated Gemma, and she had a battle to hide the irritation that unsettled her.

'You're working too hard, Gemma.' Ellen Rice had been one of her best friends since they'd entered kindergarten together twenty-five years earlier.

Gemma ignored her, pushing up the sleeve of Ellen's cotton smock to wind the dark pressure bandage around her upper arm.

'If you weren't here, people would go to Craigstown,' she continued. 'They did before!'

'Your blood-pressure's good; how are you feeling?' Gemma asked, but Ellen was not easily diverted.

'You should take every second weekend off at least,' she was saying, 'and a few extra days over Christmas. It's because you always answer that wretched pager of yours, and come when people call you, that we've all started to take you for granted.'

'I don't mind the work, El,' Gemma protested, aware of the tired, defeated tone in her voice but unable to chase it away. 'And it's only this time of the year I'm flat out all the time.'

'I know that, but it's not good for you. And we do impose on you. I didn't need to bring Roly over when he fell out of the tree, but, because I knew you'd say OK, I did it!'

'I think that's what being a local GP is all about. Old Dr Roberts always came, didn't he?'

'The town was half this size when he was here, *and* he had the good sense to go away for three weeks every Christmas, leaving the ambulance men in sole charge.'

'How are *you* feeling? was the question, not how am *I* looking!' Gemma tried to get the conversation back on to Ellen's health.

'Fat, and tired, and fed up, if you must know,' Ellen responded. 'I thought if we talked about you it might make me feel less sorry for myself.'

'Any particular physical symptoms, or is it only the fact that you're pregnant at this time of the year that's getting you down?'

'Just being pregnant full stop,' Ellen replied, surprising Gemma, who knew how much Ellen loved her children, and what a good mother she was. 'I look at you, slim and young-looking, for all your over-work, and here am I, dragging myself about the place like some great beached whale.'

'Despite your size, you still look exceptionally beautiful and you know it,' Gemma argued as her eyes took in the inky black hair and clear blue eyes of her friend. 'You've got two great kids and a husband who worships the ground you walk on, so go home and count your blessings.'

'OK,' Ellen grumbled, pushing herself up on to the edge of her chair, 'but I bet you wouldn't swap places with me for anything!'

Wouldn't I? Gemma thought The vague disquiet she'd been feeling had suddenly found a focus.

'Go home, Ellen,' she said firmly as the depression that had been creeping up on her all morning deepened. 'I'll see you next Friday, if you're still around.'

'What do you mean, if I'm still around? I've got three weeks to go!'

'I doubt it!' Gemma replied.

'I can't go early,' Ellen moaned. 'I was late with the first two, and I planned on being late with this one. Mum's gone down south to my younger sister for Christmas, and won't be back till New Year, and she's going to mind the other two while I'm in hospital.'

'I could be wrong,' Gemma hastened to assure her, 'but it's silly not to be prepared. And as for planning to be late—well, really!' She chuckled as she spoke then went on to say reassuringly, 'Geoff's mum would have Joanna and Roly in an emergency. There's no need to panic.'

'I won't go before Christmas,' Ellen repeated, backing towards the door as she spoke.

'As that's only four days away, you should be right, but don't count on anything! And make sure your bag's packed!'

'Thanks, friend!' Ellen muttered venomously as she manoeuvred her bulk through the door.

The day progressed, with Gemma deciding that it was tiredness causing her contrary mood. With a sudden determination to get her life back on track, she resolved to have a quick meal at the Fish Kettle on her way home from work, and an early night.

'What will I tell Anne Kelso?' Karen asked as she dropped the files for the three final patients on Gemma's desk.

'I'd forgotten her!' Gemma felt her brow wrinkling and her muscles contracting, but she forced herself to face the situation with professional calm.

'If I don't see her tonight, I'll have to make a time over the weekend, which I hate doing, or on Monday, which is Christmas Eve. Tell her tonight's OK, but could she leave it until eight o'clock.'

Karen's eyebrows rose.

'I told Grant I'd have dinner at the Kettle. I haven't

seen much of him lately—not to talk to—and he asked me for Christmas and I can't go,' Gemma explained. 'If I go there and eat first, then I can speak to Anne and have an early night when she leaves.'

'Bright idea! I'll let her know as soon as I've sent in the next patient. The sooner you get through them, the sooner you can get away!'

It was still close to six before Gemma finished, and she wondered if she should review her patient appointment times, in the hope that one day she might stay on time throughout the day.

With Karen and her nurse already gone, it was quiet in the little building as she washed her face and hands, then pulled her hair free and brushed it vigorously.

The face in the mirror lacked the sparkle of the one she'd confronted two nights earlier and she felt absurdly disappointed that she wouldn't be seeing Simon this evening. Then she poked her tongue at herself for being foolish, smoothed cream into her cheeks and a bright lipstick on her lips and walked back through her office towards the deserted waiting-room and the front door.

Two minutes later and she would have missed the phone call!

'It's all your fault for even suggesting I might be early. My water's broken and I'm getting terrible cramping pains every five minutes, and Geoff's in town with the kids doing their Christmas shopping and I'm too nervous to drive.' Ellen's voice rushed over the phone, her usually placid tones overlaid by a hint of panic.

'You're better going in the ambulance anyway, if the pains are that close,' Gemma assured her. 'Have a quick shower and pack a nightdress and some toiletries; I'll ring the ambulance.'

'I can't go in there on my own, and what about

Geoff? Who'll let him know?' Ellen wailed, adding a plaintive, 'Gemma?'

She didn't need to put the question into words. She needed a friend more than a doctor, and Gemma had been a friend first.

'I'll come with you,' she promised. 'Leave Geoff a note telling him what's happened and the time you're leaving. Ring your obstetrician in Craigstown—he'll alert the hospital—and, if you've got time, ring Geoff's mum and let her know what's happening. I have to make a couple of phone calls to rearrange things here. I'll tell the ambulance to pick you up first, then stop here for me. Don't panic; you probably won't progress very quickly.'

'Oh, no?' was the tart reply. 'If that's the case, I'd like to know what's happening at the moment.' She gasped into the phone, then, seconds later, added a brief, 'See you!' and hung up.

Ambulance first. Gemma dialled the number and explained, adding, 'Give her ten minutes to get organised, and don't forget I'm coming with you.'

Grant was easy. He was more concerned about Ellen than about Gemma missing dinner, and assured her they'd catch up soon. 'Come Sunday night, if you're free,' he told her, not suggesting Saturday because the restaurant was always booked up and he would be too busy to sit down for a meal.

Anne Kelso sounded aggrieved, and Gemma wondered about Karen's judgement of her. Was she the kind of woman who was charming as long as everything was going her way? Was this the basis of the marriage problems?

'I have surgery in the morning, but I'm free in the afternoon, if you could arrange for someone to mind the boys for an hour.'

'I'll have to see,' she said petulantly, making Gemma wonder angrily why she was bothering with her.

Because Simon asked you to! The answer came quickly, but it annoyed her even more than the woman's attitude. She barely knew the man, yet here she was, rearranging her life to suit him, and growing maudlin at the prospect of not seeing him for twenty-four hours!

Well, she told herself defiantly, at least I haven't been wasting my time considering his proposition. But, even as the thought flitted through her mind, the heat he was able to generate so effortlessly flooded through her body, and she knew, without looking, that the sparkle had returned to her eyes and the glow to her face.

'Damn the man!'

She walked swiftly back to the washroom, and grasped her mane of hair, plaiting it out of the way with quick movements. Just in case I have to get involved in delivering this baby, she thought, and hoped fervently that they would get to the hospital in time. Obstetrics had never been her favourite subject and, at the moment, pregnancy and childbirth, with all the associated joy and laughter, seemed exceptionally irritating to her.

The ambulance horn alerted her, and she hurried out, locking up carefully as she left. Ellen was held securely, in a half-sitting position, on the stretcher in the back and grinned weakly at her. Gemma took the attendant's place beside her.

The vehicle was so well-sprung it was hard to accept that it was moving at a fair speed, and she checked the foetal heartbeat and Ellen's blood-pressure and pulse.

'You OK?' she asked, seeing her friend twist as another contraction seized her body.

Ellen nodded, then, as she relaxed again, she smiled

and said wryly, 'It doesn't get any better with practice, this business.'

'Painful, huh?'

'The pits!' Ellen agreed. 'And if Geoff doesn't get home and get the message soon, he'll miss out on seeing this one born.'

Gemma nodded. 'Have you continued timing the contractions?'

'They're still about five minutes apart,' Ellen told her, then added, 'Don't worry, Gem, you won't have to deliver it. I'll make it to the hospital before it arrives.'

'I've delivered dozens of babies,' Gemma told her firmly.

'And you've hated it every time!' Ellen teased.

'Well, I always feel I'm intruding on something private,' Gemma tried to explain. 'That's one of the reasons I've encouraged homebirths, especially when we've got a midwife as good as Joan in town.'

'Women who have homebirths have never experienced the sheer blissful luxury of a week in hospital with people fussing over them.'

'Or they have family and friends all willing to come in and do the fussing.'

'Well, it's not for me,' Ellen assured her. 'The mere thought of my relations all being around would be enough to stop me having kids. They'd be fighting with each other, and arguing about who does what! I like the sanctuary of a pleasant birthing suite, and my husband there to hold by hand.' She paused for a moment before adding, 'But if I had to choose, I'd rather have my obstetrician any day!'

Ellen's voice faded as another contraction gripped, then passed, and she lay sweating in the temperature-controlled cabin as they raced towards the hospital.

'Do you want to lie down, or sit up more?' Gemma

asked, more distressed than she thought she would be at the sight of her friend's pain.

'I'd like to walk around, but that's not terribly practical, is it?' Ellen joked, and Gemma realised, for the first time, that, in spite of the torturous convulsions of her body, she was happy and excited.

It seemed to Gemma that Ellen had embarked on a journey to a secret place where she could not follow, and she felt a strong, stabbing pang of jealousy. I'm envious of Ellen, envious of all the women I saw today, she acknowledged to herself, both amazed and ashamed by the discovery. With a brutal honesty, she analysed the irrational distaste that had haunted her all day, and accepted the reason for it.

The next contraction was much closer—less than four minutes—and Gemma wondered if she could ask the driver to stop while she checked the dilation of the cervix. If the contractions progressed to three-minute intervals she would, she decided. She was here as a friend, because Geoff wasn't available, but it was hard to reconcile the roles of friend and doctor.

'Talk to me,' Ellen ordered, relaxing back against her support, and wiping the damp face-towel she had brought with her across her face. 'Who's the fellow you had dinner with at Grant's the other night, for a start? I meant to ask you when I saw you at the surgery, but I forgot.'

'How does the gossip spread so quickly in this town?' Gemma demanded. 'It was nearly ten o'clock at night and there was not another soul in the place, yet you've got me tabbed!'

'I don't remember how I heard, but I do remember that the report said he was some hunk!'

'Honestly, Ellen,' Gemma objected, 'it's practically indecent for a woman in your condition even to be thinking about hunky males.'

'Thinking about them is all I can do in this condition,' Ellen assured her, 'so entertain me in my hour of need, and tell all!'

'He's a visiting doctor I met at work, and he drove me out to Suzi and Michael's when my car had a flat tyre, then waited and brought me back and fixed it. The least I could do after all that was eat with the man.'

The words came out in a defensive rush, and Gemma prayed that the casual indifference in her voice would put an end to Ellen's interest.

'Is he married?'

So much for prayers being answered! Gemma thought wryly, and placed her stethoscope on Ellen's distorted stomach to evade answering, then watched her rhythmic contraction distort the swollen shape once again.

'You didn't answer,' Ellen accused her when it had passed, and Gemma shook her head. She'd never been any different, friend Ellen! She'd keep asking until she got an answer.

'No, he's not,' she said briefly, 'but don't go getting any fancy ideas about pairing us off. He's a specialist with what I imagine is an extremely lucrative practice in Melbourne, and I'm settled where I am, thank you. It's what you might call geographically impossible, even if either of us was interested.'

'But you could have a little fling with him, surely?' Ellen suggested. 'A nice, safe holiday romance!'

'Ellen!' Gemma cried, so loudly that the attendant spun around in his seat. 'She's fine,' Gemma assured him, then bent low over her friend to hiss, 'How could you even suggest such a thing? And what's happened to all your high moral attitudes? Poor Geoff wasn't allowed more than a chaste kiss until after you were engaged! If this is what marriage and a family does to you, maybe it's a good thing I stayed single!'

'You could do with some fun in your life!' Ellen asserted. 'You don't want to end up a dried-up old maid without even one great romance to look back on. And don't tell me you had one with that Alex,' she added, 'because he was the most selfish and self-absorbed man I've ever met, and I'm sure it would have been reflected in his lovemaking.'

Gemma glanced quickly towards the front of the ambulance, fearful that Ellen's voice would have reached the two men. They were talking easily—about horse-racing, she discovered as she leaned forward to eavesdrop. Nothing would have penetrated their concentration on their sport, she decided, breathing a sigh of relief.

She looked back at her friend, but her eyes were closed and she was breathing with quick, shallow gasps. They were on the outskirts of town and would make it to the hospital. Maybe the pains were close enough now to distract Ellen from her 'friendly' advice session.

She had enough trouble with her wayward body pushing her towards further contact with the visitor, without Ellen adding her voice to the promptings.

Gemma pushed her way out through the heavy doors at the entrance to the maternity wing of the sprawling hospital building. She paused for a moment, and breathed deeply. Doctors should come to life when the unmistakable odours of a hospital entered their lungs, but it was something she had never accepted. The mixed odours of antiseptic, human bodies, clean linen, and the indefinable taint of fear or apprehension in the air had always disturbed her, and she was grateful that her hospital work was minimised by distance.

She breathed deeply, savouring the heady scent of

gardenias, and her eyes picked out the well-pruned bushes lining the pathway back to the road. Tall lamp-posts threw the path and the bushes into sharp relief, the flowers brilliant white against the almost black-green of the leaves. She moved towards a bush and breathed in the fragrance to dispel the hospital smell from her nostrils.

Geoff had arrived in time for her to leave Ellen before the baby had been born, and she had waited only long enough to hear that it was a little girl, and plant a congratulatory kiss on Geoff's cheek, before fleeing the place. The ambulance had gone straight back, and she could wait an hour or two and get a lift back with Geoff, or. . .?

There was no alternative, apart from a cab, and no driver would be happy having to drive out to the Bay this late in the evening! She moved restlessly along the path, and then back again towards the door. Apart from anything else, she was hungry!

She could go and visit Gavin Wells while she waited—but that would mean going back into the hospital, and first she'd have to burst in on Ellen and Geoff to tell him she was waiting. . .

'Like some company, lady?'

The voice came out of the darkness beyond the lamp-posts, and she spun around to see a tall, familiar figure striding across the grass towards her.

Her heart reacted with a peculiar little skipping beat, and her stomach somersaulted.

'What are you doing here?' she demanded suspiciously, angry now that the object of her earlier distraction had appeared in person.

'I've been to visit my patient, and saw you pacing the footpath like an expectant father. How's your friend doing?'

'How did you know——?' she began, then realised

the answer. She'd told Anne where she was going and why. 'She's had the baby, actually, and I've been trying to decide whether to wait for the proud father to drive me home or get a cab.'

She was talking because his nearness made her nervous, and she didn't want it to show, but the words were ill-advised, as she realised as soon as they popped out of her mouth.

'I'll take you home,' he said swiftly, as she'd known he would. 'Have you eaten, or shall we grab a bite here in town before we set off?'

'I can't keep eating with you,' she muttered crossly.

'Oh?' he queried quietly. 'Is there a rule against it?'

She looked up at him now, and felt the strange melting sensation in her bones as she saw the twinkle in his pale eyes and the creasing lines of humour in his cheeks.

Why wasn't he married? she thought, then wondered why she should be thinking such a thing!

'There's a good Indian restaurant on the way out of town, if you like that kind of food,' she said ungraciously. 'And I'll pay!'

He nodded and smiled genially. 'You'll feel much better when you've eaten. I've noticed how hunger tends to make you tetchy.'

She opened her mouth to protest, then bit back the furious retort she'd been about to utter. Why give the man more ammunition?

'The car's over here,' he said smoothly. 'I'll drive and you direct me, and we'll be tucking into a delicious meal in no time at all!'

He took her arm, as he had done so often before, and guided her back across the grass towards the car park.

CHAPTER EIGHT

'How's your patient?' Gemma asked, when the serious business of ordering a meal had been concluded.

The ensuing silence made her look more closely at her fellow diner, and, even in the dimly lit restaurant, she could see concern tugging his brow into a frown.

'Worried about him?' she asked, sensing real anxiety.

'I shouldn't be.' He sighed. 'But I've got a funny feeling about him.'

'Is that why you drove in to see him even though you'd handed the case over to the registrar at the hospital?'

'No,' he replied abruptly, as if his patient had been the last thing on his mind when he'd made the decision to come to town. 'But, having seen him, I feel uneasy.'

His fingers had been moving restlessly, picking up the cutlery and rearranging it. Now he bowed his head to watch them as they attempted to balance his knife on the tines of his fork. The task absorbed him, as if this small feat of manual dexterity might provide an answer to his problem.

'Is there something specific bothering you?' Gemma asked, watching those long, lean fingers with a hypnotic fascination.

She saw the movement of his body as he shrugged, and waited patiently, beginning to know this man who would choose his words carefully.

'There's more pain than I would have expected at this stage—a deep, throbbing pain unconnected with the tissue damage.'

'And?' Gemma probed gently.

His balancing act forgotten, he looked up at her and almost smiled, his eyes twinkling in a way that was becoming too familiar for her peace of mind.

'What do you remember about compartment syndrome?'

'I thought that was more likely to occur with closed fractures,' she responded, searching rapidly through her memory bank for more information. 'Pressure builds up within one of the compartments of the limb, and, because the fascia does not stretch with the swelling, blood flow is reduced and dreadful things can happen. Surely, in an open fracture—'

'Judging by what you've seen, not what you know, Doctor, dear?' he warned, and Gemma's mind went blank.

It was his continued use of meaningless endearments, she decided, that threw her out of kilter! What was he saying?

'It was a crush wound, not a complex fracture,' she amended slowly, thinking it through, 'but it was still open.'

'Which meant that the lateral and anterior compartments were both damaged, but what about the posterior?' He looked across the table at her and smiled, shaking his head in mock-reproof, yet, in spite of his making light of it, she sensed his anxiety.

'What can you do? How can you know what's happening in there?'

'We can measure the compartment pressure now. I've spoken to Sinclair and he's prepared to do a fasciotomy if it goes above 30mmHg.'

'So?' she asked with a smile.

She had his attention now as he looked up into her eyes, and the smile became a warm and genuine response.

'So what?'

'So why, rather,' she teased. 'Why are you worried?'

The answer was a long-drawn-out sigh.

'I suppose because he's not officially my patient and I'm not his doctor, and I won't be doing it, and, being only human, I believe I'd do it better than anyone else in the whole world. Then there's the fact that I don't want it to happen because it's an added complication the poor kid doesn't need and will prolong the healing time of the open wounds and all sorts of things. . .!'

The rush of words petered out like a mechanical toy that had run out of power, and he grinned again, slightly shamefaced after the abject confession.

Gemma felt the charm of the man firing every tiny cell in her body, and flustered into speech to hide her reactions.

'And here I am envying your professional detachment!'

'Practice doesn't always follow theory,' he said wryly. 'Just as knowing right from wrong doesn't always make decisions easier, Gemma,' he added, with a depth of meaning in his voice that made her shiver.

Decisions? She had promised him a decision! Could she plead his own argument, that it was night again and one should never make decisions at night?

'Saved by the food, sweet Alice,' he murmured, as if he had followed every twisting strand of her wayward thoughts.

Simmering dishes of aromatic food were placed on the table between them, and Gemma's mouth watered as she savoured the spicy, tangy scents of the offerings.

'Go to it!' Simon ordered as he bent to examine the different delicacies. 'This must be the chicken tikka,' he pronounced, 'and this the lamb korma. Kashmiri pullao, is easy, and the aloo mattar is this potato and pea curry.'

He smiled at her, that teasing twist of his lips that plucked at her heart-strings and sent her pulses racing. With a calmness she was far from feeling, she spooned a little of each dish on to her plate, adding a crisp pappadom to the selection.

'It seems we're always eating together,' she murmured to fill the silence that was spinning into a tight thread between them.

'There's a certain intimacy in sharing food!' He caught the conversational ball with his usual ease and sent it hurtling back into her court. 'Think of the Roman bacchanals, wild orgies of food and wine that ended in long nights of love.'

'Love or lovemaking?' she replied with some asperity. 'I think there's a difference.'

'Semantics, Gemma? Shall we play with words?' He was spearing a piece of meat with his fork as he spoke, and she saw him hesitate, then raise his eyes to question hers.

'I think it's better to play with words than with feelings,' she muttered, disconcerted by the feeling of entrapment that engulfed her. It was as if she were a fish, hooked, but not yet landed by a consummate angler, and she doubted her ability to win the battle that was taking place between them.

'Why are you so afraid of what you feel? You trust your impulses, intuition—feelings—if you like—in your work. You must do, or you wouldn't be a good GP. Yet in your emotional life you distrust those same spontaneous reactions.'

As he spoke, in a quiet, unemotional, conversational tone, Gemma ate, barely tasting the delicious flavours as her mind sought the words she needed to refute his arguments.

'You know nothing about my emotional life,' she said, falsely calm!

'I know you're attracted to me.'

'So?'

'So what are you going to do about it? It's decision time, sweet Alice.'

'I've already told you,' she said crossly as her heart thudded against her ribs, almost suffocating her with its extreme reaction. 'You're looking for a nice, light-hearted affair and I'm. . .' She paused as she realised what she would like to say, and hurriedly sought an alternative ending. 'Too busy!' she finished lamely.

Simon continued eating, and for a moment Gemma thought she might have escaped the line that held her to him.

'Too busy or only interested in long-term commitment?' he mused, still absorbed by his food, and speaking so quietly that he could have been talking to himself.

Gemma ignored him.

'Do you ever sense life passing you by, while you wait in your fairy-tale world for that perfect, perhaps unattainable dream?'

Now he looked at her, and the lack of laughter in his face, the lightless intensity of his pale eyes, sent a shiver of dismay through Gemma.

'It depends what you call life, I suppose,' she countered valiantly, refusing to be intimidated by his word play. 'My life is completely satisfying for me, although I can understand someone of your sophisticated tastes soon tiring of its simple pleasures.'

'Nothing missing, Gemma?'

Of course there is, she wanted to cry, but what you're offering isn't the answer.

'No!'

The word reverberated in the air between them, denying its truth in the very strength of its delivery.

'Your nose will grow,' he said calmly as he placed

his fork carefully on his empty plate and sat back with a deep sigh of satisfaction.

Gemma felt tiny flickers of anger flaring to life deep inside her as this man calmly destroyed her peace of mind and poked and prodded his way into her subconscious, arousing feelings she did not want to acknowledge and doubts she did not want to feel.

'I think you're the one having trouble with reality, Simon Griffiths,' she argued crossly. 'You're the one who keeps resorting to fairy-stories in your conversation—maybe your life's the same. Your idea of happiness seems to revolve around having fun! Nights at the theatre, brief affairs and let's never get heavy or serious! If that's how you see life then maybe it is passing me by, but all I can say is good luck to it, because that isn't what would satisfy me!'

'Do you want more than a brief affair?' His eyes met hers across the table, met and held them until she had to look away!

The question took her breath away. What was he asking? The words were coldly unemotional, lacking even the friendly interest she usually found in his voice. Exasperation joined the anger!

'How can we possibly have anything other than a brief affair?' she demanded, her voice rising shrilly. 'You're up here on holiday for however many more days or weeks—I don't even know that! You live in Melbourne, for heaven's sake! It's impossible. You're impossible!'

And now he had the temerity to smile! Her fingers curled around her fork as if it had become a weapon, and she stifled an overwhelming urge to fling it at him.

'Eat up,' he ordered. 'We've a fair drive still ahead of us.'

With a ragged, despairing sigh, Gemma obeyed him, finishing off the delicious food with little appreciation of its taste or texture. She'd escaped from his line, hadn't she? She'd told him in no uncertain terms that she wasn't having an affair with him! Then why had he smiled? Why did he seem to think he'd won? And why did she feel so flat and miserable?

She paid the bill, but the satisfaction she should have felt in that simple act was missing. It was as if the repayment of the meal had somehow ended their relationship. There was no longer a reason for them to meet again—to share another meal. She'd miss the curious camaraderie that had sprung up with such ease between them—miss the medical rapport as well—and his easy smile and teasing conversation!

'The car's out this way,' he whispered in her ear as she stood by the reception desk and counted her regrets. His hand grasped her arm, proprietorial yet protective, and the warmth of it sent a burning fever shimmering through her body like a forest fire.

Why did you smile? she wanted to ask, but the strong feeling of relief that had flooded through her when the conversation had closed made her unwilling to reopen it. She waited while he unlocked the car, fighting the fever that burnt in her veins like the heat of the summer sun, and quelling the riotous impulses that danced in the skin he had touched.

They drove in silence along the narrow road back to the Bay. The darkness of the eucalypt forests pressed close against the road, making the headlights spear ahead of them like twin beams in a long tunnel. The big vehicle took the steep climb up the range with ease, then glided round the first few turns on the descent towards the town, before swinging off to the left, into the picnic area, which, in daylight, looked down across the coastal strip.

'Is something wrong?' she asked, waking from the

half-doze into which the smooth journey had lulled her.

'No,' he replied, staring out through the windscreen towards the lights of the town below them, and the palely gleaming sea.

'Then why have we stopped?' Somewhere deep inside her a warning bell had clanged—even before she asked the question—but Gemma failed to recognise it for what it was.

'We're parking,' he said calmly.

'Parking?' she shrieked. 'What do you mean, parking?'

'I mean parking,' he repeated. 'It might be called something different up here in New South Wales, and the young kids probably have another name for it, but back in my youth it's what a boy and girl did on the way home from a night out.'

He ignored her gasp of surprise, and, with unhurried deliberation, undid his seatbelt and reached across to curl an arm about her shoulder.

'You stop at a place with a nice view like this,' he continued, as if explaining something to a four-year-old, 'then you move a little closer together, like this——' he negotiated his way across the gear lever until his leg lay alongside hers, bombarding it with messages she did not want to recognise '—then you have a bit of a kiss and a cuddle.'

And with that he swung her body round towards him, and bent his head to kiss her lips.

Trapped by her seatbelt, there was little Gemma could do—although as she told herself later, there was probably plenty she need not have done. Her lips responded to the touch of his with a hunger so intense it was almost pain. They claimed the softness of his mouth, and rubbed against the bristling line above and below as they twisted, seeking to relieve some of the yearning she could not acknowledge.

She felt his mouth open slightly as he whispered her name, and her tongue, tentatively trying out a new game, flicked across the inner moistness, then tangled with his in a joyful frenzy. His hands caught in the plait of hair that hung down her back, and, even as their lips clung, she felt his fingers moving, releasing the confining band, and running through the long, soft tresses, so that it streamed around them both as they clung together.

Now there was a growing urgency, and hands and lips became more searching, more insistent, touching, feeling, kneading, smoothing, nibbling, tasting, sliding! She felt his skin beneath his shirt, and quivered as his fingers brushed her breast. Her breathing deepened, quickened, and fluttered from her lips as his hands tempted her body beyond all common sense and reason.

A strangled groan brought her back down to earth as she felt the warmth of his body move away, leaving her cold and shaken.

'Bucket seats are no good for parking,' he said, his voice rasping breathlessly into her ear.

Shaken by the tumult he had aroused, Gemma sat in silence, adjusting clothes, and pushing her hair back over her shoulders. She breathed deeply, in, out, in, out, hoping that hyperventilation might still her racing pulses, and cool her flushed and heated body.

'Why did you smile, back there in the restaurant?' The words popped out as if propelled by some force outside her mind, which still refused to function on a rational level.

He turned towards her, his profile clearly defined against the moonlit sky, for a long moment, she thought he would not answer. Then, finally, she heard the words, murmured almost inaudibly as she strained to hear.

'You said a lot of things about time and distance and impossibilities, but you didn't say no!'

'I meant to say no,' she whispered.

'Did you, Gemma?' he breathed, firing the engine and swinging the heavy car back on to the road.

If he kisses me again when we get home, I'll give in, Gemma realised fearfully, recognising that her body had already made the decision her mind refused to contemplate. She peered through the side-window into the darkness, unwilling to look at the man who was disrupting her life with his presence in this town, and tempting her body with his subtle magic.

He did not speak again, nor did he touch her, but her mind continued to argue with itself as she battled to control her own impulses. Slowly, another realisation seeped into her consciousness. If he doesn't kiss me, I'll probably kiss him!

The thought shocked her so much that she shut off her mind, breaking the silence with an inane remark about the number of cars still about as they drove through the town.

'I cannot make a commitment to you, Gemma,' he said very quietly, ignoring her attempt to change the conversation and answering her own chaotic thoughts.

'I understand that,' she told him, hearing a degree of despair in his voice and wanting to reassure him. The tension in the car was almost palpable as he turned from the main road and drove with great concentration past the surgery and up the long hill towards her house.

'No, you don't!' he told her as the car pulled up outside her sheltering bank of greenery.

It no longer matters, she wanted to cry, but words that had never been spoken before were hard to say, and she merely turned to him and reached out to touch his arm.

'Are you coming in?' she asked, knowing he would understand that this was her decision.

'Oh, sweet, sweet Alice!' he murmured, looking down at her with a curious, twisted smile on his lips. His arm grew rigid beneath her fingers, and the air between them vibrated with a now acknowledged need. The darkness hid his eyes, but she felt their close regard, then the sensor lights sprang up in the dark foilage, and Grant appeared on the path that led from her house.

'Not tonight, it seems, dear Doctor,' Simon said, his voice as hard as the eyes that were now clearly visible in the bright floodlights. He reached across her frozen body, and opened the door, leaving her no alternative but to climb out, shaking with tension, despair and frustration, as the stupid game they were playing was unresolved once more.

'What on earth are you doing here at this time of night?' she snapped at Grant as she slammed shut the door of Simon's car and listened with a sinking heart as it turned and slid away down the hill.

'I wasn't sure how you were getting back from town, and thought I'd better check that you were OK. I also wanted to hear about Ellen. I've been dozing on your veranda.'

He made no mention of her chauffeur, although his gaze had followed the car down the hill.

'Simon was in town seeing the lad who was injured on the trawler. Ellen had a daughter, Geoff got there in time, and all is well.' She spoke with an unaccustomed curtness, aware of it, but unable to control the disappointment that prompted it. 'I'm sorry if you've been waiting long, but we had a meal on the way home.'

It occurred to Gemma that he must have closed the restaurant early, or left someone else in charge, to be here at this hour—a little after ten—but she was too confused to follow the thought through to any rational conclusion.

'I'm sorry I had to miss dinner,' she continued, wishing he would say something, or go away, 'but I couldn't let Ellen go in on her own. She was prepared to panic because the baby was a few weeks early. Would you like a cup of coffee?'

Even as she asked the question, she hoped he would say no, not because she was tired, but because she suddenly, desperately, wanted to be alone. She rather thought she might like to cry, or maybe laugh hysterically. . .

'I won't stay! I can see you're tired and not interested in talking to me.'

He sounded huffy, but that was another thing she was unable to think about at the moment. Her own behaviour was causing enough confusion without tackling an analysis of Grant's moods and actions.

'I'll see you in the morning, then,' she said a little too warmly as her relief was translated into gratitude.

'Will your doctor friend be there?' he asked as he walked past her towards her carport where his car was hidden in the shadows of the tall palms.

Startled by something in his voice, she looked after him, her mind swinging into action.

'I don't know,' she grumbled, 'but it's a public beach. He's entitled to walk on it if he chooses!'

The shrill ringing of the phone brought her instantly awake, out of an uneasy, restless sleep. Grey lightening of the bedroom's darkness heralded the dawn, as she answered the call and listened to the agitated woman on the other end.

'I'm sorry to bother you, but I know he's going into shock; I've seen it before. I told him it would happen—it's the holidays, and the weather——'

'Tell me your name and where you're staying,' Gemma broke in, hoping the woman would respond to her calm voice.

'Miller, and we're at the Grange motor inn, unit seven. He's a diabetic; it was the beer for sure!' The woman's voice had a righteous edge of blame to it, her earlier panic slightly allayed now that she had handed her problems over to Gemma.

If it was the beer, it's more likely to be hyperglycaemia, she was thinking as she pulled on a skirt and T-shirt and pushed back the tendrils of hair that had escaped her plait during the night. Her mind, as usual, raced ahead, rehearsing possibilities and planning to meet them.

She had glucose and insulin in her bag anyway, but if it was diabetic ketoacidosis he would have to go into town to hospital where his blood glucose and ketone levels could be monitored hourly and his electrolyte and acid-base balance checked frequently. She'd know when she saw him and could call the ambulance from the motel, she decided as she hurried down the hill to the surgery and her car.

The big man on the bed hadn't lapsed into a coma, but his pulse was weak and rapid, and one sniff of his breath confirmed the diagnosis that his dry, flushed skin and restless agitation suggested.

'I'll give him insulin now, but he'll have to go into hospital in town for a few days. They can continue with a continuous low-dosage intravenous treatment until his levels stabilise, and monitor the effect of the treatment.'

The woman nodded as if she had been expecting this.

'It's happened before. We try to take our holidays in the winter months. That way it's not hot and he doesn't feel like an extra beer! This year we came at Christmas because our kids wanted to holiday with their friends, and he only had a few beers. . .'

She paused, and Gemma wondered how many was a 'a few'! She drew insulin from the vial into a syringe. 'What medication is he on, and when was it last taken, do you know?'

'He's on thirty units of insulin a day and usually has one slow-acting injection in the morning, then a faster-acting one later in the day.'

'He tests himself?' Gemma asked, and watched the woman nod.

'Could he have forgotten the second injection?' she asked quietly, knowing the woman was not to blame. Educating the patient to balance their carbohydrate, fat and protein intake and to monitor their own condition was the most important part of treating an adult diabetic, and the man must have been aware of the risks he was taking.

Again the woman nodded.

'Would you phone for an ambulance?' she said, speaking gently now as she moved towards the bed, where the man tossed and muttered confusedly. 'When he's ready to travel, I'll start a saline drip to help replace his fluid balance, and the attendant can monitor it.'

She watched as the woman dialled the emergency digits and spoke into the phone, her voice calmer, accepting the inevitable now that she had some medical support.

'I'll pack his spare pyjamas and toiletries,' she said with resignation as Gemma explained to the man what they were arranging for him. She checked his pulse again, and then his blood-pressure, noting down the figures on the report sheet that would go with the ambulance. The attendants would add anything that might happen on the journey then pass it on to the medical staff at the hospital. Carefully, she noted the amount of insulin given and the time, then added a note about the 'few beers' of the previous evening.

By the time the ambulance arrived in Craigstown, the patient should be rational enough to tell the staff exactly how many 'a few' had been, and also when he had last taken his medication.

'How old are your children?' she asked as the woman came back to stand beside the bed and reach out for her husband's hand.

'They're fifteen and thirteen,' she replied. 'Old enough to take care of themselves for the day. I'll wait till they're up and have had breakfast, then drive into town and stay with Don for the day. Our friends will keep an eye on them.'

Gemma nodded, then moved towards the door as she heard the ambulance pull up outside the motel unit. Behind her she heard a deep murmur of regret and a softer voice reassuring, comforting. For better or for worse—that was what marriage was all about, she conceded with a sigh. Even if the 'worse' was self-inflicted, the love and forgiveness remained the same.

'Starting early these days, Gemma?' Ken Williams asked as she let him and his offsider in.

'And how,' the responded with a smile, suddenly aware of her tangled hair and hastily flung-on clothing. 'You're not the only one who heaves a sigh of relief when the holiday season is over.'

The two men wheeled the adjustable metal-framed stretcher over to the bed, and lifted the big man on to it with ease.

'I'll see to the kids and come in later,' the woman whispered, her voice thick with tears now that the emergency was under control. 'Thank you so much for coming. Do I pay you now?'

'I want to set up the drip before they go,' Gemma told her, seeing the woman's distress. 'Why don't you call at the surgery one day next week? I'd like to hear how he's getting on.'

'I'll do that,' she replied. 'Now I'd better have a shower and get dressed before the kids are up and about,' she added, hurrying off to hide the emotion she felt.

'You coming with us?' Ken asked as they wheeled their patient carefully out.

'Not this time,' she said, handing him her record sheet and walking beside the man as he was moved, 'but I'll attach him to a drip once you've got him strapped in. I thought I'd use the saline from your kit as my supply is running low and who knows what will happen next!'

'Bludger!' Ken replied as he climbed up into the cabin of the ambulance and held out a hand to pull her in.

'Well, you can replace yours at district headquarters when you get in there!' It was an old argument that Ken expected of her, and interaction that added to her job satisfaction.

Sitting at her patient's side, she found and checked the solution she needed, then, with, precise attention, attached and flushed the tube, applied a pressure bandage, then inserted a catheter to take the fluid directly into the raised vein. Hooking the fluid reservoir into position above the patient, she smiled down at him and patted his arm.

'You're on your way,' she said cheerfully. 'I hope they won't keep you long, but, if you come back here to finish your holiday, please keep off the beer!'

He responded with a weak grin, but his colour was more normal and his skin cooler to the touch.

'And you're lucky your wife is a light sleeper,' she muttered as the ambulance pulled away.

'Talking to yourself? It's a bad sign!'

The big car had been hidden by the bulk of the ambulance, and she flushed as she saw Simon's unsmiling gaze flickering over her untidy hair and dishevelled clothing.

'What are you doing here?' she demanded, her heart palpitating with a frantic irregularity that left her weak and shaken.

'I missed you on the beach this morning,' he said softly, not moving from his perch high above her, 'then when I saw the ambulance I guessed you might be near by and thought I'd wait and see.' He paused for a moment, looking down at her with an expression she could not read in his pale eyes. 'I wanted to talk to you about something,' he added.

'Talk?' Gemma echoed, shivering slightly as warring emotions splintered her mind and body. She was conscious of dismay that he should see her like this, yet filled with an incongruous delight that he should want to see her—and devastated by her body's response to his presence.

'Medical talk,' he said roughly, reading her reactive shiver as distaste. 'I thought of something that might interest you.'

The words were as effective as a bucket of cold water, but she was saved from replying when Grant walked past towards his flat a little further along the esplanade. He called a coldly polite, 'Good morning,' to her and continued on his way, not pausing to enquire where she'd been or join in their conversation.

She watched him go, her eyebrows knitting as she

puzzled over the peculair behaviour he'd been exhibiting lately.

'Is Grant someone special in your life?' Simon demanded, shocking her with the question. There was a curious rasping edge to the words, and an intentness in the eyes that watched her warily.

Wheels whirred in her mind and several unusual, unrelated occurrences clicked into place, forming a picture she did not like. Surely not, she thought, then realised she hadn't answered Simon's question.

'No!' she muttered, blushing as she spoke, denying his assumption and her own sudden, and unwelcome, insight. 'He was waiting last night to ask about Ellen.'

'I wonder?' Simon replied, nodding as if in confirmation of his own thoughts.

'Grant and I have known each other since pre-school,' she told him crossly. 'There is not, and never has been, anything more than friendship between us.' She took a deep steadying breath, then added defiantly, 'Not that it's any of your business.'

'Of course not,' he replied lightly.

As he smiled down at her from the high window of the car, she felt her anger melt away, and smiled back, feeling a unique sense of peace settling about her like a benediction.

'Do you want a lift home?' he asked, his voice a strangely suggestive whisper that shafted through her body like a flood of irrational despair!

'I've got my car,' she muttered. 'It's late! I've got to get to the surgery! I can't. . .'

'It's not that late, Gemma!' was all he said, switching on his engine and pulling out of the motel driveway, leaving her standing on the pavement with her heart twisting inside her as the car disappeared from view.

CHAPTER NINE

ONCE again, heavy footsteps announced Simon's arrival as Gemma dressed after a quick shower. She'd been disappointed earlier, when she'd arrived home and found he wasn't here, yet now his presence caused uneasiness.

'I've brought breakfast; shall I put the coffee on?'

Excitement and apprehension warred within her.

'I can do it,' she protested weakly. 'I'll be out in a few minutes.'

Had she known—hoped?—he'd come? The glowing colour in her cheeks and unmistakable light in her soft brown eyes seemed to suggest it. Smiling ruefully at her reflection, she nodded slowly. How often did she wear her patterned linen mini skirt and matching silk T-shirt—clothes that emphasised her slim figure, tanned legs and glowing golden colouring, and made her feel deliciously feminine—to work?

With a smile she could not banish still lingering on her lips, she smoothed on a light creamy make-up that also provided maximum protection from the sun's UV rays, then highlighted her eyes with a muted brown shadow, darkened her eyelashes, and picked up her hairbrush. She'd put on lipstick after breakfast, she thought as she brushed through the tangles.

'Coffee's brewing!'

With a feeling of dismay, she watched her reaction to his voice, seeing, in the mirror, the physical signs of the tumultuous excitement his presence engendered with such effortless ease. Grasping her swath of hair in one hand, she pulled it forward over one shoulder, and plaited it loosely, so that the colour and shine were evident in the soft folds, and silky tendrils fell about her face, softening the regular features into a kind of beauty.

'Croissants and coffee,' he announced as she walked through to the dining area. 'That do?'

The words might have been mundane, but the low-pitched timbre of his voice enriched them with secrets that made her shiver in apprehensive delight. How could she keep pretending? How long would she be able to maintain this façade of calm control when her body was alive with an unbelievable desire to be near him, with him, touching and clinging, feeling, learning, knowing?

'It sounds delicious,' she said carefully, blushing under the appreciative glimmer in his eyes, and maintaining control over her speech and breathing with the greatest difficulty.

If he'd walked on the beach with her health walkers, he must have been home and showered after it, for there was a freshness about him that she could see, and almost feel. His long, loosely knit body was clad in crisp white shorts and a pale blue and white cotton shirt. The colours accentuated his tanned skin, and deepened the colour of his eyes. Long hours of work had not made him soft, or pudgy, she decided, seeing the firm delineation of muscles in his forearms, and the faint bulge of solid flesh beneath the sleeves of his shirt.

'Do I pass?' he asked, placing a warmed roll on a plate in front of her with a devilish grin.

'You look fit enough for someone who works in an office or hospital all day,' she conceded casually, hiding her embarrassment with quick words.

He passed the butter, carefully cut and set on a small dish he must have found in her cupboard, then offered jam. Her gaze followed the movement of his fingers, as if mesmerised by their presence at her table. She'd seen them working with such delicate precision on the leg of the injured boy; had felt them coaxing her body into a frenzy of delight. The thoughts brought a rush of hot blood through her veins and bright evidence of this warmth to her cheeks. She forced her mind back to practicalities. He was a colleague, she reminded herself—a colleague and nothing more!

'You wanted to talk?'

'I did,' he agreed and smiled at her, his lips quirking with a sincerity that made her forget her resolve. 'Remember you were talking about the young girls and your doubts about the availability of oral contraception?'

She nodded, her mouth full of buttery flakes.

'Well, I remember reading somewhere of special clinics set up for teenagers, both male and female, to deal with their specific problems.'

'Like family-planning clinics or women's health centres?'

'That type of thing!'

'Family-planning clinics do handle contraception and many young girls use their services,' she told him, dubious of the value of what he was suggesting.

'Yes, but most are put off by the name! And what young man wants to enter such a place? The mere thought of planning a family must make him shudder with fear!'

Something in his voice as he spoke of family rang so true that her head jerked up, to see if she could catch a clue to his emotion in his face, but his eyes were lowered and his hands relaxed as he toyed with his knife to occupy fingers that could not be still. She remained silent, shaken by the unspoken intimation.

'You'd have to find a trendy name that would appeal

to adolescents, or you'd never get them in, but it could be an after-school drop-in centre with a variety of services offered. If three or four medicos volunteered their services, say for three hours one afternoon a week, young people could go to them with their concerns and questions.'

'So, providing we all agree in principle about our approach to teenage problems, girls that see me for their tetanus needles here would be able to see another female doctor in town?'

The idea began to take root in her mind, and grew with surprising speed as she considered the possibilities.

'And what about the young men who don't want to discuss their doubts and insecurities about sexuality with a woman they probably fantasise about?' he queried with a lifted eyebrow and a gleam of laughter in his eyes.

'I'm hardly the stuff of fantasies,' she argued, and ignored his murmured demur, 'but I know the young lads hate having to come to me for anything that requires them to take their clothes off!'

Concentrating on his idea helped to keep her mind off his attraction.

'It would also solve the doubts the teenagers must have about whether or not I'll tell their parents of their visits—not that I would, of course.'

'Even though you'd like to at times?'

'Even though I sometimes feel I should,' she defended, knowing how torn apart she felt when confronted with the problem.

'What's worrying you now?' he asked, reaching across the table and covering her fingers with his warm hand.

'I'm thinking it through,' she replied, hoping she was

concealing the pleasure his gesture gave her. 'What makes you think I'm worrying?'

'Your eyebrows twitch together like this!' He frowned ferociously to illustrate his point and she chuckled, seeing the creases in his cheeks deepening to dimples as he joined in her laughter.

'Would I be passing the buck? Abrogating my responsibility with the excuse that I didn't know what was going on?' She felt her eyebrows twitching together once again and hoped she didn't look as fierce as he had suggested.

'Gemma, Gemma, Gemma!' he cried, throwing up his hands in horrified surrender. 'If you agonise this much about every decision you make in your life, I'd need a three-year holiday to talk you into a little light romance—although I did think I sensed a weakening last night.'

He smiled at her so sweetly that she felt her heart lurch in her chest. For a fraught instant she thought he might press home his point, but, instead, he kept talking about the embryonic idea.

'You have to go back to the basic requirement that all those participating will be in agreement on ethical values and the kind of service you want to promote. That agreement will include an understanding that under-age patients should be persuaded to be as open with their parents as they feel is possible. It's all you, or anyone else, can do.'

Smiling at him, she nodded again. 'It's a great idea. I'll try to put the concept into words and circularise the GPs in town who might be interested. Once we have a core group willing to give time to it, we can contact the others and ask if they would be willing to support us by advising parents and younger patients that we exist.' Her mind raced away as the possibilities for future inclusion of counsellors, career advisers, therapists and dieticians promised a unique service for the young people of the surrounding area.

'I'll have to ask the council about premises,' she muttered, following her thoughts to the exclusion of all else.

'Whoa there.' Simon brought her sharply back to the present as his hand closed over hers once again. 'It's Saturday morning, then the Christmas break! The councillors are all at home relaxing!'

She had to chuckle at the words. 'You're right,' she admitted. 'And I've got to get to work. We'll talk more about it later.' Even as the words issued from her mouth, she regretted them, and rushed into speech again to try to make amends.

'I'm sorry. I didn't mean to sound as if I expected you to be here, or that you had to waste any more of your holiday time talking about this. It was a great idea, and I thank you!'

Heat was rising in her body as she stumbled through the embarrassing apology, and she knew her turmoil would be evident in her cheeks.

'I'd willingly spend my entire holiday listening to your ideas and discussing the centre with you, but. . .' His fingers left hers, reaching out to select another croissant, and his head bent as be broke it open. Something in his carefully controlled movements cooled her heated blood more effectively than any words, and she waited tensely for what he was about to say.

'This breakfast is a farewell of sorts,' he said finally, when his croissant was prepared to his satisfaction, and his fingers had stilled above his plate.

'Farewell?' The words came out as a pleading denial, as if she hoped he hadn't said what she thought she'd heard. She looked up at him with a kind of dread. Last night she had been prepared to give in to the demands of her body—demands that were as urgently insistent in the cool light of this new morning!—and now he was saying goodbye.

'Anne's husband turned up last night—unexpectedly, of course! He's handed all his patients over to another specialist and taken an extra week of holidays to try to work things out with her.'

'But that's great,' Gemma said quickly, forgetting her earlier panic as she thought of the woman who had briefly been her patient. 'They can't hope to achieve anything while they remain apart, and if he's not working they'll have the time to talk things through and see where they can go from here.'

'I do agree,' Simon told her, but the rueful smile on his face made her wonder what was coming next. 'The problem is that I'm definitely not needed, decidedly *de trop* in fact. . .'

'Oh!' Gemma remembered her own interpretation of Simon and Anne's relationship. 'I can see it could be awkward!' She grinned at him, pleased that he seemed disconcerted about the situation.

'I took myself off to the Grange motor inn last night—which is why I was there this morning,' he confessed, 'but, with Christmas Eve on Monday, Tuesday Christmas Day, and Wednesday a public holiday, they are booked solid for the next week. They rang around all the other motels and the hotel, but there's not a bed to be had.'

'You've strayed out of your fairy-stories into the world of the biblical, haven't you, with this "no room for him at the inn" fantasy?' she said, her voice strained as she realised what he was saying.

'I have rather, haven't I?' he replied, grinning at her with such shamefaced complicity that she felt her bones melting. Then the grin faded, and the light died in his eyes as he said seriously, 'Unfortunately, it means I'll have to cut short my stay here.'

Her stomach twisted with a raw anguish that she had never experienced before and she felt her fingers trembling as she tried to maintain her composure. Clasping them tightly together beneath the table, she spoke with as much restraint as she could muster.

'But what of your holiday? Every town on the coast will be the same! Where will you go?' A giant hand seemed to have gripped her intestines, and was squeezing hard, while every muscle in her body was tensed against the knowledge that he was leaving.

'I'll head south,' he said calmly. 'I've friends in Sydney who'll have me!'

'You could stay here,' she whispered, her eyes glued to the plate in front of her so that she would not see his reaction to the rash offer that had sprung her lips. 'As a colleague, of course,' she added quickly, wondering if he could hear the tumultuous thudding of her heart against her ribs.

'So, in the evenings we could have deep philosophical discussions about common thyroid problems and the treatment of piles?' he said lightly, and she looked up at last to meet his eyes that were still and watchful.

'There's a spare bedroom,' she said flatly, knowing she was repeating an invitation that should not have been offered, but knowing also that she couldn't bear for him to leave—not yet!

'You should think it over a bit more, Gemma,' he said quietly. 'I appreciate your offer and would love to stay, but, however platonic it may be, the town will assume we're having an affair, and it will reflect badly on you,' he pointed out, his face carefully masking his feelings.

She nodded, knowing with absolute certainty that she should retract the offer right here and now, then add goodbye and wave him on his way. It was the answer to her problems, the solution she had prayed would appear. Once he was out of town, she could relax, and life would soon return to normal. Soon? Well, eventually!

'Think it over,' he repeated, standing up and clearing the dirty plates from the table. 'I'll call back this afternoon. What time would suit you?'

Her mind seemed to regain a vestige of control as he spoke, talking about time as if it were a patient she had agreed to see. His back was turned towards her as he walked across to the sink, and she found herself studying its broad strength as she thought.

'I'm not certain,' she mumbled, as backs and time and his leaving threw her mind off course again. 'I thought I'd get my hair cut when I finish work, if I can get an appointment. It will depend——'

He spun around and faced her, and she forgot what she was saying as she saw what looked like shock and horror on his face.

'Don't get it cut,' he begged, surprising her so much that she gasped as she looked up at him. She watched his cheeks darken as colour must have flooded under his tanned skin. 'None of my business,' he muttered, turning away again and running water into the sink to wash the dishes.

'You can't hang around all day while I think!' she objected, trying to ignore his reaction to her remark about a haircut.

'I don't want to leave, Gemma,' he said, with a peculiar emphasis of the word 'want'.

'Then maybe you'd better stay tonight,' she said, trying to dispel the strained uneasiness that had suddenly permeated the air around them. 'I'll try to think of something that might suit you, and we can talk about it over dinner.'

'Shall I book somewhere for us to eat?' His voice was muffled as he bent over the sink, taking an inordinately long time to wash two plates.

'Of course not,' she said quickly. 'I can cook, you know! I've a small lamb roast in the freezer; we'll have that.'

'I'll see you later, then,' he said, still not turning around.

Was he afraid she'd see something in his face? she wondered uneasily. Was this just a ploy to inveigle his way into her bed? She drained her coffee and shook her head, frustrated by her thoughts. I asked him to stay last night, she argued in her mind. If Grant had not been waiting on my doorstep, we'd have been breakfasting together as lovers.

'You'll need a key to get back into the house if you go out; there's a spare on a row of pegs by the door.' Her voice was tight, forced out through lips that were stiff with the tensions building up between them.

She'd have to find somewhere else for him to stay if his presence in the house made her feel like this.

'I won't stay. It was wrong of me even to consider it,' he said suddenly, swinging around to face her with a face as impassively unrevealing as a wooden mask. 'Presumptuous, that's what it was. I had no right to put you in this position, to make you feel obligated.'

'Don't be ridiculous,' she snapped, relieved that the tension seemed to have broken, but dismayed by his words, and devastated by the thought of his leaving. 'If you want to stay on at Grange Bay, you're more than welcome to stay here.'

Gemma had a distinct impression that something beyond her control was making the decisions, and forming the words that she had spoken. She looked up at Simon, his figure dark against the light from the kitchen window, and tried to read the expression in his shadowed eyes.

'I doubt we'll stay platonic friends, sweet Alice,' he said at last. 'When you first suggested it, I told myself it would be possible, but when I see you, feel your nearness in the air about me, hear your voice curling into my ears I know I want more!'

He walked across the room towards her, as if drawn to her side by an irresistible force, then stopped on the far side of the small table, and leaned his hands on the edge of it as he looked down into her eyes.

'Send me away, Gemma,' he warned. 'It's the wisest course. I'm not the man for you. I can offer nothing more than a holiday romance—the one thing you don't want! But I don't think I'm strong enough to do the right thing—to walk out of here and never come back. You'll have to send me, Gemma. You'll have to tell me there's no point in my staying.'

He was so close she could hear him breathing, and feel the air that he expelled brushing against her skin. His eyes glittered with an almost feverish intensity as she felt him trying to will her to do as he commanded.

'We'll talk tonight,' she muttered, pushing herself up from the table, forcing her legs to carry her wayward body away from him.

'Gemma!'

She turned towards him, keeping the table between them, but it might as well have been invisible for he bent across it, towards her, his body warming hers with its pulsing arousal. His hands hung loosely by his side, as if he was forcing them to relax, then they moved, reached out, and grasped her elbows, and his dark head lowered to hers as her lips parted to receive his kiss.

As naturally as drawing breath, her body responded, her mouth opening like a flower to the morning sun as his tongue slid across the silky moistness on the inside of her lips, tantalising her with its tenderness. Her hands slid up against his chest, and felt the hammering of his heartbeats against her fingers. The blood sang in her veins as she sensed his heated response. His kiss, his hands, his body seemed to be telling her the one thing that his lips would not say—that there might be love where he saw only need.

What do you know about love? one tiny functioning portion of her brain asked sarcastically, but she was too lost in the emotional upheaval of his embrace to follow the question to any logical conclusion.

His lips left hers as suddenly as they had descended, and she bowed her head as she dragged air into her lungs and fought to regain some shreds of composure.

'You do see what I mean,' he muttered, sinking back into his chair. His voice sounded harsh, hardened by anger, but whether it was directed at her or at his own lack of control she could not guess.

'For heaven's sake, I'm neither a child nor an idiot,' she retorted. 'You don't have to keep repeating that all you want is a bit of fun. I understand that—I should,' she added, her voice rising as the frustration she was feeling found an outlet in anger, 'you've told me often enough. No commitment, no commitment; it's like a spell you whisper to protect yourself. I accept that, so why the hell can't you accept that I know the consequences of my decision?'

She spun away from him, then turned back, gripping the edge of the table to control the shaking rage that coursed through her. 'Why shouldn't I have an affair if I want one?' she demanded defiantly, then caught the gleam of laughter in his eyes and her temper erupted. 'And it's not funny!' she yelled as her hands lifted, and she tipped the remnants of their breakfast—coffee-plunger and mugs, butter dish and jam jar, croissant crumbs and sugar bowl—neatly into his lap.

Why shouldn't I have an affair? The question recurred throughout the morning, although she felt the subject had probably become academic. His friends in Sydney would seem welcome relief after this morning's débâcle. She had left without another word, without a backward glance, teeth-cleaning and lipstick forgotten as her righteous indignation had carried her out of the door, into the car, and down to the surgery, still fuming at the man's contrary behaviour.

Why should she be the one to make all the decisions? If he'd wanted to go, he should have gone. He owed her nothing, no apologies or explanation, so why hadn't he packed up and left? He'd have found someone in Sydney to satisfy his needs, without the slightest problem, she decided, thinking how easily he had charmed her. Yet the thought of him out with someone else brought back the anger.

'You're bright and early this morning,' Karen greeted her.

'I started early.' Gemma explained about her early morning call, pleased that her voice sounded calm and rational. 'You might ring the hospital for me later and check on his progress, Karen. Any problems I should know about for this morning?'

'Not a one, and a nice light schedule. We saw all the regulars during the week. Allan Kerr rang. Jimmy's asthma's bad this morning and he's bringing him in, there's a holiday-maker who's let a foot wound get infected, Mrs Spring for her iron injection, the Baker twins for their second triple antigen, two unknowns who rang for appointments but didn't say why and that's the lot, barring emergencies.'

'I hope it stays as quiet over Christmas,' Gemma

said as her mind welcomed the relief of normal procedures to blot out the confusion that beset her.

Allan Kerr, a man who juggled his work as the engineer on the local council and his responsibilities as a sole parent, with great skill, entered the waiting-room, with Jimmy and his sister Sharon in tow.

'Come straight through,' Gemma said, waving her hand towards her office door as Karen neatly cut Sharon out of the little procession with a colouring book and pencils.

'Problems, Jimmy?' Gemma asked the small boy as she opened the file that was sitting ready on her desk.

'Been eating too much junk food, I guess,' the boy replied, and Gemma could hear the rasping wheeze in his voice.

'It's a tough time of the year,' she said sympathetically, then asked, 'Have you got a sore throat, cold, sniffles, earache?' knowing that any infection could trigger Jimmy's condition.

'No way, I'm healthy,' he assured her, shaking his head at the thought of a germ daring to enter his body!

'Then I'd better listen to your rattles and squeaks, hadn't I?'

The freckled face lit up with a wide, cheeky grin, and Jimmy pulled up his T-shirt to reveal a thick, tanned chest.

'Still swimming?' Gemma asked as she picked up the constricted bronchioles.

'Yes, but training and club swimming has stopped for the holidays—'

'So it's just surfing, and occasional afternoons at the pool,' his father interrupted. 'Do you think that's a problem?'

Gemma smiled at his anxiety but was quick to relieve it.

'Not at all,' she told him, then adjusted Jimmy's shirt

and patted his arm reassuringly as she added, 'But with the excitement of Christmas, and the unseasonal dry, windy weather, it's not surprising you're a bit off-colour.'

He grinned at her, sensing she was an ally against his father.

'Dad's been wanting me to keep up my training,' he admitted.

'And it wouldn't hurt you,' Gemma told him with mock-severity. 'But, as it's holidays, I suppose you could slacken off. You're having your Pulmicort every morning and evening?' she queried, and received a confirming nod. 'Then go on to Ventolin four-hourly today, and see if that helps. Keep right off milk and cheese and ice-cream, and take it easy. If you're still coughing or wheezing tonight, then you'll have to go back to the nebuliser four-hourly for a few days.'

Jimmy responded with a deep groan, but Allan nodded, as if Gemma's words confirmed what he had thought. His hand rested on the boy's head protectively and Gemma felt again that tug of envy she had experienced the day before when her pregnant women had reminded her body of its biological functions.

'It's just Christmas,' Allan said abruptly, and Gemma nodded, knowing that he had provided an excuse for her own emotions with his explanation. The children's mother had been killed driving back from town doing her last-minute Christmas shopping, a year before Gemma had returned to Grange Bay, but she understood how deeply her loss must be felt at this time of the year when families celebrated their togetherness.

'Do you need a new prescription for the Ventolin or Atrovent solutions for the nebuliser?' she asked, unable to voice the sympathy she felt for him.

'No, thanks, Gemma; I keep a supply on hand, just

in case. I'd have done as you said, but I wanted to be sure.'

'I'm not going away over Christmas, so if you need me please call,' she said as they left the room. 'And Merry Christmas!'

'Same to you, Dr Wainwright,' both children chorused as Sharon seized her father's hand and proceeded to drag him out of the door.

The words echoed hollowly around her office. If she hadn't tipped the breakfast dishes all over Simon Griffiths this morning, she might have had a merry Christmas and happy New Year, and to hell with commitment, and possible heartbreak, and future regrets!

Mrs Spring came tentatively through the door, following Karen, who dropped her file on Gemma's desk and departed. The elderly lady smiled shyly at Gemma in spite of the fact that she'd known her since she was born. Some of the older inhabitants of Grange Bay retained a caution in their approach to her that made her wonder if they doubted her ability.

'How are you, Mrs Spring?' she asked brightly, knowing it was a stupid thing to ask a patient, but unable to come up with anything better. 'Your blood-pressure's down this month, which is good,' she added, checking the notations her nurse had made on the file.

'I'm fine, Gemma,' the elderly woman replied, fishing in her old brown handbag for a beautifully wrapped gift. 'And this is for you,' she added with a smile, 'to say thank you for being such a good doctor, and for coming back to Grange Bay. How I'd hate to be going into town on the bus every month for my injections. You've no idea how easier you've made things for us oldies!'

'Don't think I came back for you,' Gemma joked as she prepared the Vitamin B 12 injection that held her patient's pernicious anaemia in check. 'I found I couldn't live anywhere else. It's I who should be thanking you for making it possible for me to earn a living in the place I love best.'

Resting the syringe in a kidney dish, she dipped a cotton swab in alcohol and asked, 'Where do you want it, thigh or rump?'

'Thigh, please,' was the reply, as certain as the sunrise. Mrs Spring belonged to an era when women didn't bare their buttocks in front of anyone, even other women!

She swabbed the wasted muscle and slid the injection in, knowing it would be better in the other site, but unwilling to offend this old friend by forcing the issue.

I do belong here, she reiterated to herself as Mrs Spring made way for Sarah and John Baker, each bearing a nine-month-old baby. Mrs Spring's little gift, sitting prettily on her desk, forced treacherous thoughts of Melbourne from her head.

The morning passed, and, with it, the panic she had felt when she had first arrived at work, after fleeing the house, and its occupant, and all the demons he had awoken in her mind and body.

'Three to go,' Karen informed her cheerfully as she dropped two thin files on the desk and left a cup of sweetened coffee and two biscuits beside her blotter. 'I'll give you five minutes before I send in the next one, so drink that in peace!'

'Five minutes' peace?' Gemma joked.

'Well, it's better than nothing!'

Karen whisked back out of the room, and Gemma reached for the coffee.

He was the last 'patient', coming into the room with the shamefaced expression of a little boy caught out in some mischief. It didn't detract one jot from his appeal.

The sight of his tall, rangy body constricted her bronchioles far more effectively than Jimmy's asthma had affected him!

'I couldn't just walk out of your life!' he said, as if the words would make perfect sense.

'I'm sorry about this morning,' she muttered, knowing that her eyes were saying what her lips could not. Please stay, she felt them pleading, and saw the answering shake of his head.

'I shouldn't have laughed at your temper tantrum, but I had to laugh or kiss you again, and, if I'd done that you'd never have made it to work this morning.

She saw his face crease into the so-familiar smile, and the white teeth gleam with his self-derogatory amusement.

'Will you stay?' she asked. Her gaze wandered over him, as if memorising features she would never see again, taking in the unruly wave in his hair, probably longer now than he wore it in the city. His eyes were calm, hiding his thoughts, and there was a tiny piece of skin flaking at the end of his nose, where he'd been burnt a few days ago.

His lips moved but she didn't hear the words, her mind absorbed with imprinting his image in her memory.

'I said, would you move to Melbourne if we found we wanted more than a brief affair?' he repeated, when she came back to earth and begged his pardon.

The words rang in her head. Was he offering her commitment or simply a longer liaison at no cost to his own comfort or security? Did it matter?

No! her body cried, but her eyes found the tiny Christmas package on the desk and, with a painful slowness, she shook her head. 'I belong here,' she told him gently.

'Then I'll be off,' he said, standing up and walking

towards the door. Then he paused, and her heart stilled its racing beat as he turned to face her once again. 'I love your long hair, Alice,' he murmured, and left.

She felt bereft!

CHAPTER TEN

THE hot summer days dragged by, as record-high temperatures produced an enervating lassitude and dry, scorching winds which scraped nerves raw. The older locals talked about the seasons changing, and reminisced about the days when a cyclone in the north would bring torrential rain to the coastal strip, and promote a muggy, sultry, humid heat far different from this current weather pattern.

The holiday crowds were gone, but Gemma found she was still busy as the unseasonal weather sent the population seeking relief in unorthodox ways that meant she had a spate of silly accidents and minor emergencies to keep her mind off her own unhappiness.

Grant had shocked her out of her misery for a brief interlude, when he'd declared his love for her and proposed. Upset by the thought of hurting her old friend, she'd actually considered his proposition for a split-second, then realised that both of them deserved more than second-best. But his departure for Europe for his 'working-holiday' had left her lonelier than ever.

As each day dragged towards the next, she waited for the aching sense of loss to diminish, and for the memory of the love-affair that wasn't to fade and die. She chided herself on her stupidity when footsteps on her veranda made her heart race, and forced herself to see the beauty of the early morning which had dimmed without him by her side.

We did too much together, she thought crossly as

she drove out to Orana one evening, fighting the man's persistent ghost.

'Young Mark's stopped the dreadful coughing,' Michael greeted her as she crossed the veranda to the kitchen door. 'Suzi has him in the bathroom with the hot shower running like you said.'

'I can't think why we missed a humidifier when we ordered the list of paramedical supplies you might need,' Gemma replied, handing him the box she had tucked under her arm. 'If you set this up in his room, I've some vaporising liquid in my bag that you add to the water. The instructions are on the bottle.'

Ros appeared in the kitchen and Gemma smiled at her as she asked, 'You have got a nebuliser, haven't you?'

'Would that have helped?'

'No, steam's the answer and the shower is the next best thing to a humidifier, but I'll give him a single dose of racemic epinephrine which should reduce the swelling in his throat and help him over this more quickly. Did he show any signs of an infection earlier today—sore throat, mild fever or a runny nose?'

Ros shook her head. 'He's such a wild kid,' she said, 'I doubt anything short of a train engine would stop him. I'll get the nebuliser.'

Resting her bag on the table, Gemma found the small vial she needed, and a new face mask. Michael handed her Mark's file and she looked through it.

'He's diagnosed as having attention deficit disorder, but this ADD seems to be the label doctors are putting on anything they can't pin down to something else,' he told her as she leafed through the pages.

Gemma nodded agreement as she emptied the vial into the small plastic reservoir and attached the tubing and mask.

'Could you carry this through to the bedroom?' she

asked. 'And I'll rescue Suzi and the patient from their foggy environment.'

The little boy looked sleepy now, as if the battle to breathe had finally sapped his over-abundant energy. He sat on Suzi's knee, his thumb in his mouth, sucking gently as he looked at Gemma with dazed blue-green eyes.

'We'll take him to the bedroom,' she murmured. 'Michael has the humidifier going in there.'

She followed Suzi out of the room, fighting the thoughts of Simon that the boy's pale green eyes had awoken.

'Leave it on all night,' she advised the houseparents as they watched the boy drift off to sleep, his breathing eased by the drug and assisted by the moist air. Suzi nodded.

'The other kids are all in bed; will you stay for coffee?' Michael's suggestion warmed her, and she realised she was in need of company.

'That would be great! I'd like to check Mark again in an hour, if you can put up with me for that long.'

'Considering we haven't seen you since Christmas Day, we'll be delighted,' Michael assured her, hurrying ahead of them to put on the kettle.

'Have you heard from Simon?' Suzi asked quietly, pausing in the darkened room, her hand on Gemma's arm to detain her for a moment.

Gemma shook her head. 'I didn't expect to, Suzi,' she replied, pleased that the gloom would hide the twisted pain she felt at the mention of his name. She had poured out her heart to Suzi on Christmas Day, when the misery of Simon's departure had hung like a thick cloud around her head, blotting out the bright happiness of the festive occasion.

'You could have contacted him,' her practical friend suggested.

'I might have, I suppose, but I saw his friend again between Christmas and New Year—eager to try nicotine patches to stop smoking now she and her husband had sorted out their problems!'

'She stopped you getting in touch?'

'Hardly!' Gemma said drily. 'She was unaware of anything between us—enmeshed as she was in her own misery. Simon could have vanished in a puff of smoke and she wouldn't have noticed!'

'Then what happened?'

Gemma sighed, then decided she'd have to continue. 'She's a chatterer, and somehow, during the course of the conversation, she managed to give me a run-down on his parents, who were both "marry-ers."'

'"Marry-ers?"?' Suzi sounded astounded.

'They split up when Simon was very young, and kept remarrying and divorcing at regular intervals. According to his friend, Simon had four stepfathers and three stepmothers by the time he was sixteen, and the constant shuffling completely disillusioned him about the concept of marriage, and destroyed any belief he might ever have had about commitment.'

'So it was an affair or nothing?' Suzi asked, the sympathy in her voice weakening Gemma's resolve to shed no more tears over the infuriating man!

She sniffled back the moisture and said firmly, 'There was no future in it, Suzi. Quite apart from his obsession about long-term commitment, there's a little problem of distance. He's a specialist! It takes years to build up a successful practice like his.'

'You could have moved to Melbourne!'

'For what? A chance to fall more deeply in love with the wretched man? To have more memories later when he said, That's it? I don't think I'm strong enough for that, Suzi!'

'Coffee's ready!'

'I'd go,' Suzi declared as they walked slowly towards the kitchen. 'I'd go and enjoy whatever he could offer.'

'And to hell with tomorrow?' Gemma asked wryly, knowing that Suzi was putting her own strong inclination into words.

'Why not? You've only got one life!'

The conversation ended as they entered the brightly lit room, and Michael passed them mugs of steaming coffee. Gemma sniffed at the rich, aromatic brew, and thought of the breakfast she and Simon had shared—breakfast—and dinners—and moonlight. . .!

Ros was talking about the dreadful weather, and Michael was asking if she could remember it ever being like this before, but her mind had drifted away and was lost in memories of moonlight.

'There've been several small brush fires round the base of the hills lately,' Michael was saying as she dragged her mind back to the present.

'I wonder if the smoke triggered Mark's croup?' Suzi asked, but Gemma shook her head.

'The dry weather and smoke are affecting the asthma sufferers and people with sinus conditions have been miserable, but Mark has probably some low-grade infection,' she explained. 'If you could bring him into the surgery tomorrow I'll check his ears and throat, and maybe start him on antibiotics. He wasn't hot, but you never know with kids, their temperature can shoot up so rapidly.'

'You sound as if the unseasonal dry spell's been keeping you busy,' Michael said sympathetically. 'Maybe it's time to be looking for a partner.'

Gremma stared at him, wondering how much Suzi might have repeated.

'The practice isn't big enough for two people,' she protested.

'Are you certain?' Michael persisted. 'Have you

looked at your workload lately? Really analysed it, and thought about the population increase, and the men who still go to Craigstown because they want to see a male doctor?'

'And the extra work you'll be doing in town when your teenage clinic gets going?' Suzi added. 'You should think about it!'

'I'm too tired and too busy to think at the moment,' Gemma said weakly.

'Which proves our point!' Michael announced triumphantly.

It was Suzi who changed the subject, diverting the attention away from talk Gemma wished to avoid, but their suggestion lingered in her mind as she drove home later. If she had a partner, it would make for a smooth transition if she left. The treacherous thought crept into her mind!

But how could she leave! The Teenseen clinic was due to open in a fortnight and initial reaction to the idea had been overwhelmingly enthusiastic. She would have to see it through its infancy. It was a bad time to be thinking about getting a partner, but maybe, when it was up and running, she'd do something! With a partner, she could take a long holiday, and. . .!

Smoke from the dampened fires hung in the air as she drove through the darkness, and she blessed the stillness of the night. Dry winds now could whip them back to life, and, with the forests tinder-dry, bushfires were becoming a serious threat. She thought of the small volunteer fire service, and made a mental note to check on her emergency supplies—especially plasma and saline—just in case!

As she came into the lights of the town, she smiled at the twist her thoughts had taken. Grange Bay still clung to her like an old and favoured garment!

* * *

The dry north-westerly winds came a week later, whipping across the wide continent, bringing dust and the deadly sparks of dry electrical storms. The fires started on the far side of the range, and no one worried. It had happened before, but the fire brigade in Craigstown would handle it. The real danger was still fifty kilometres from the little sanctuary by the bay.

Housewives complained about the soot and ash that marked their washing, and filtered into the house to leave greasy black stains when they tried to wipe up.

Gemma, driving home from her final pre-opening visit to the rooms where she and five other young doctors had set up their Teenseen clinic, saw the glowing colours on blackened tree-trunks, and the fiery flaring embers deep in the bush-covered mountains. Smoke formed a blue cloud in her headlights, but the flames were still far from the road, and on the western side of the low range of mountains that sheltered Grange Bay.

She woke next morning to an unbelievable scene, as a blood-red sun glowed in the dark, thick atmosphere. She knew the fires must be closer. Her house was the last one on the hill, and the bush crowded closely above it. Aware of the dangers, she'd had a strip of land between her house and the forest cleared and sown with grass, which her regular gardener kept mown and clear of debris. Her rainforest planting was another protection, its lush moistness far less flammable than the eucalpyts which many gardeners in the area favoured.

She rang Bob, who headed the volunteer service, and his wife confirmed what she had suspected. The fires were out of control in the ranges and if the wind continued Grange Bay would be in the path of the raging conflagration.

'You know what to do,' Betty said calmly, and Gemma agreed, although the hand that held the receiver was shaking. 'Check the gutters are clear of leaves, push rags into the down-pipes and fill the gutters with water.' She recited off the drill she'd learned in Bob's lectures of bushfires.

'Then play the hose over the roof and back of the house, and, if you're going out, close all the doors and windows,' Betty reminded her, then added, 'If you're coming down into town to work, Gemma, you should pack a small bag with spare clothes and toiletries in case it does cross the hills and you don't get back up there for a while.'

The thought of leaving her precious house to the whim of the fire's path filled her with dread, but she accepted the sense in Betty's advice. Knowing she could be called out at any moment, she hurried through the basic tasks, then packed a bag and drove away, unshed tears pricking behind her eyelids.

She drove first to the school, where she learned the high-school bus had left early and got through to town, although the road was now closed and the students would have to be billeted in Craigstown until the fires were under control and the road cleared of fallen trees.

'I'm going to contact all the parents and send what kids are here home,' Doug Jenkins, the headmaster, told her.

'While your staff are phoning, may I speak to the classes?'

'Sure can. I'll take you round myself.'

Starting with the infants, Gemma moved through the school, talking calmly to the pupils about precautionary measures, and reminding them of the rules if their house caught fire.

'Get down low and go, go, go!' a bright seven-year-old told her, showing she had learned her lesson when Gemma and Bob had visited the school at the end of the previous year. If the fires came down into the town, she hoped the entire population would be gathered on the wide curve of sand where the river flowed out to the ocean. Even with the town's limited facilities stretched to the limit, the fire would be stopped by the green expanse of playing fields and picnic grounds that bounded this stretch of beach.

'Mr Jenkins is going to send you all back home soon,' she told them, smiling at the delighted response that the news of this unexpected holiday received. 'But I want you all to take home some important messages to your parents.' Tongues stilled and wide eyes looked up at her. This was responsibility indeed!

'First, tell them you should be wearing little masks to keep the smoke from making you sick. You can use a handkerchief, like this—' she held up a large square and folded it to a triangle '—and tie it around your nose and mouth like this. It works best if you wet it, and keep it damp,' she added as she removed it, and grinned at the children's excitement.

'Also, tell them to listen for the siren. If the men from the state emergency service think the fire's getting close, they'll sound the siren at the top of the ambulance tower. When you hear that, you know it's time to pack up a few things in your schoolbag and go down to the reserve. You should take a blanket each. All of you are big enough to carry your own blanket, aren't you?'

Little heads nodded, and Gemma smiled. The state emergency service was another volunteer organisation, formed after disastrous floods ten years earlier, and Gemma had worked closely with them as they'd made contingency plans for emergencies like this. While she was speaking, other volunteers were checking the stockpile of food and medical supplies in the big SES shed down on the reserve.

Her pager told her that she was wanted at the

surgery, and she hurried through her visits to the older classes, knowing Doug would reinforce her message before the children were sent home.

'We're actually handling your patients extremely well,' Karen said cheerfully when she arrived at work. Two volunteer fire-fighters were sitting in the waiting-room wrapped in blankets, with loose, dry sterile dressings covering the burns on their arms.

'But she won't give us a cup of tea until you say it's OK!' one complained, as Gemma lifted the dressings and checked the reddened, blistered but superficial burns.

'You can have something better than a cuppa,' she joked, 'but don't go back to the front until you've had a few hours' rest. When you get tired, you get careless,' she reminded them, seeing the strain in their red-rimmed eyes and blackened faces. 'You're all supposed to be wearing woollen shirts with buttoned cuffs,' she reproved them. 'What happened to that little rule?'

'It got so hot, we pulled them off and worked in T-shirts,' one of them admitted, and Gemma had to laugh as she saw the contrite expression on their faces.

'When did you have your last tetanus shots?' she asked, then sighed as they shook their heads in bemusement. 'All you volunteers are supposed to keep them up to date,' she scolded. 'Come through, both of you. I'll give you shots and check your pulse and blood-pressure while Karen mixes you a drink.

'The lemon sodium mixture we were talking about,' she said to her receptionist as she led the patients through to her office. They were two of the men who continued to see their male doctor in Craigstown although their wives and children came to her. Keeping the two of them together might allay their concern about a female administering to them.

Karen brought in the drinks as Gemma prepared the

tetanus boosters, and she handed one to each of the men.

'Drink it down, then you can have that cup of tea,' she said firmly, while Gemma explained the importance of replacing the salts and fluids which their body tissues had lost as the processes to prevent infection and promote healing began automatically when the injury occurred.

The two men drank obediently and stoically accepted the tetanus shots before Gemma uncovered their wounds once again and felt the inflamed tissues surrounding them.

'If I ask you fellows to stay home, will it have any effect?' she asked, then nodded as both shook their heads.

'We'll have a sleep,' the older one assured her, 'because we've been up all night and wouldn't be much use out there now, but if the fire's still burning later we'll go back.'

'It's our town!' the other added, as if that explained everything.

'That's what I thought,' Gemma said resignedly. 'Well, take Panadeine for the pain but not more than four-hourly. I'll have to wrap your wounds so you don't reburn the same skin. I'll use moist dressings saturated with silver nitrate, and then wrap dry bandages around those for extra protection. But I want you both back here for me to re-dress them some time tomorrow, understand? If you get an infection in those burns you'll be very sore and sorry for yourselves and could even lose some movement in your arms.'

Both men nodded, as if impressed by the severity of her tone, then sat patiently while she bound up their arms.

'Woollen shirts!' she called after them when they

left, clutching prescriptions for broad-spectrum antibiotics in their hands.

The morning was well under way!

Many patients had cancelled appointments, and many people did not turn up, forgetting inessentials in their anxiety to make their homes as safe as possible in the face of the approaching fire, but volunteer fire-fighters suffering from smoke inhalation, eye irritations or minor burns kept her busy.

At midday, she left the surgery to set up a makeshift casualty station at the school, which had become the nerve-centre of the relief operation. The ambulance came and went, ferrying the fire-fighters with minor injuries. Gemma treated them and made them comfortable, grateful for the help of the women who had come in to prepare meals to be sent out to the men, make cups of tea, and take on nursing duties.

Early in the evening the wind swung around, and for a while it looked as if the town might be saved, but the relief was short-lived, and the effect of the sudden shift disastrous! Three fire-fighters had been trapped as flames turned back on them.

The men were brought in after midnight, and Gemma knew she had to get them to hospital. With the help of her own nurse, she searched for unburnt areas, seeking veins to start fluid resuscitation. The ambulance attendants had provided oxygen, and these two trained helpers continued to monitor the patients' airways while she cut away the burnt clothing and examined the injuries.

'Should we use ice?' one helper asked, but Gemma shook her head.

'Where possible we flush minor burns with water, which reduces the heat and the pain and clears away burnt skin and debris, but with these three it could cause a worse drop in their body temperature and we'd be risking hypothermia. At the moment, our main aim is to keep them warm and treat the shock, which is more life-threatening than the burns.'

Checking the degree of the injuries, and the extent of the burnt areas, she grew increasingly uneasy.

'Just cover the burns loosely with dry sterile dressings,' she told another helper who had nursed for years before retiring to Grange Bay. 'I'll be right back.'

Ted Rose, the Bay's only policeman, was standing by the door, and Gemma hurried towards him.

'Is the road clear?' she asked, knowing it was unlikely.

Ted shook his head, his face grey with fatigue after a night spent with the fire-fighters and a day moving elderly people from their homes to younger families who would assist and care for them if evacuation became a necessity.

'What about the helicopter?' Gemma persisted.

'There's no visibility, Gemma. Nil! Even in daylight, with the updraughts from the fires and the thick pall of smoke, he couldn't come in!'

'I've got to get these fellows out, Ted. They've got first- and second-degree burns to more than fifteen per cent of their bodies, and one chap has circumferential burns on his wrist and arm and another could lose movement in his hand. I think he needs an allograft to save muscle and tendon constriction. They need attention in a proper burns unit as soon as possible!'

'Then pray for the wind to change,' the exhausted man said, slumping into a chair by the door as the futility of the situation hit him.

Gemma hurried back to her patients.

If they were staying here, she decided, they would need pain relief. She'd start with 2mg of morphine and see how that worked. She could repeat the dose two- or three-hourly as required. She'd have to check with the ambulance men about their stock. Fluid replacement was the most important thing for the men at the moment, but burns needed specialist treatment!

While her fingers went about their tasks with an automatic efficiency, her mind raced. There must be a way to get them out!

Sam!

Back she went to Ted, shaking him roughly by the shoulder to wake him up.

'Are the fishing boats in or out?' she demanded, and watched as Ted forced his brain to work.

'They must be in,' he said, 'because Sam and some of his boys were helping down at the SES shed a few hours ago.'

'Can you get on to him and ask him if he could take the *Fan* out with these three fellows on it? If he's well out to sea at first light, the helicopter can winch them up on stretchers from his deck. With the westerly blowing, the sea must be calm.' The words tumbled out as she considered all aspects of the idea. 'Would a helicopter be quicker than one of the coastguard boats?' she asked, and received a confirming nod as Ted grabbed the idea and swung around to hug her.

'You're a genius, lass,' he said, and headed out of the door, his powerful two-way radio already crackling as he started the arrangements rolling.

Back with her patients, she administered the painkiller then prioritised their needs. She began work on the man with the burnt wrist, anxious to assess the degree of the burn as the dangers of eschar acting as a tourniquet rang in her brain.

'How does it feel?' she asked the man, gently touching the bright red skin.

'Bloody awful,' the man grunted, and Gemma smiled.

'You don't know how good that is,' she said. 'A

third-degree burn destroys the nerve-endings and isn't nearly as painful. From the look of this, it's only a first degree, which hurts like hell, but will be healed up in a week.'

She checked his pulse and blood-pressure and was relieved to see that both were stabilising, although he had first- or second-degree burns to both arms and legs, about twenty-five per cent of his body, she estimated, using the Rule of Nines. She would classify him as moderate, she decided, but close enough to critical to need hospital care.

'Stay there and stay warm,' she said, smiling down at him before moving aside to tell the ambulance attendant what had been decided, and to advise him that the oxygen mixture could be cut back to fifty per cent.

She walked across to the man with the badly burnt hand and administered morphine before she touched the wound. Using slightly dampened sterile gauze pads, she separated each finger then wrapped the weeping, red skin lightly in a dry dressing. Silver sulphadiazine cream would be soothing but she was reluctant to use anything on the wounds while there was a chance that she could get them to hospital within the next few hours.

The third fire-fighter was sitting up joking with one of the helpers by the time she reached his side.

'I was behind the other two as it came over,' he explained. 'They ducked, so my face copped the flash of hot air, and it burnt off my hair. I'm not as bad as I look, Doc!'

From the strength of his voice, he was right in his self-diagnosis. Smoke inhalation had probably affected him badly for a while but one hundred per cent oxygen had soon reoxidised his blood and the superficial burns would not require surgery or special treatment. She examined his head carefully but could see no blisters or broken skin.

'Can you walk?' she asked him as Ted came hurrying towards her.

'Sure can,' was the cheerful reply.

'Well, take yourself outside to the taps and put your head under the water for a while. It will soothe the pain and wash off all the burned hair and soot and we'll be able to see where we are.'

She turned to her helper. 'You go with him, Helen. When he's finished, pat the skin as dry as you can, bring him back here and wrap that blanket around him again—I don't want him going into shock after I've got the other two out!'

'Sam's standing by and the chopper's all fixed,' Ted announced as he reached her side.

'That's great,' she told him. 'I'll organise the ambulance men, if you could get back on to the helicopter and tell them there will only be two patients to go. Barry Cox is OK.'

Ted hurried away, and Gemma organised the evacuation, pleased to know that the men were on their way to specialist care.

'Have you had anything to eat or drink lately?' a familiar voice asked as the ambulance drove off.

'I can't remember,' Gemma said as she swung around to see Mary Parsons standing behind her. 'And what are you doing here?' she demanded, thinking of Mary's heart.

'I'm fit as a fiddle,' Mary delcared. 'Dave's been up baking all night, and I've been delivering bread to the SES hut and here for sandwiches.' She looked hard at Gemma as she spoke, and added, 'And now that I am here I'm going to see that you have something to eat. You look as if a puff of wind would blow you right away.'

'I could do with a snack and a bit of a rest,' Gemma admitted, and walked with Mary towards the tables that had been set up at one end of the big hall. 'What's the latest on the fire?'

She felt a vague surprise that for the last few hours she'd had no idea of the progress of the disaster that was threatening the town.

'It's crossed to this side of the slopes, but, with the lighter winds at night and the protection the mountains themselves provide, it's slowed a lot. The problem is, with the darkness and the smoke they can't water bomb the deep gullies. All the men can do is keep it at bay where they can, and hope the winds don't get up strongly in the morning.'

'One good gust and it can come sweeping down into town,' Gemma said, the words dragging out as tiredness and despair filled her body.

'It's not like you to be pessimistic,' Mary rebuked her. 'It's possible a south-easter could swing it back on itself, and the town would be saved!'

'I'd settle for the wind easing so it can be held at bay,' Gemma said with a smile. 'I won't expect miracles.'

She slid into a chair at one of the tables and watched as Mary went off to get her some tea and sandwiches. She'd just rest her head on the table while she waited. . .

'I'm the relief doctor,' a deep voice was saying, and she knew it was a dream and tried to stay asleep, because he seemed so close in the dream. 'Why don't you lie right down on one of your little camp beds and sleep properly for a while? I'll mind the shop!'

She could feel his hand, warm and comforting on her back, and tried to capture his face in the dream.

'I'll carry her,' the voice said to someone else, and she

was lifted into strong arms and held closely against a broad chest, and for some reason all her senses screamed, 'Simon,' although she knew it was impossible.

'I'm all right,' she said, her voice tight with disappointment as she struggled against the arms that held her. She forced her eyes open, rubbing at the stickiness that had been gumming the lids together.

'Hello!' he said very softly as he cuddled her closer and walked towards the beds.

Her dazed mind remembered the fantasies he'd woven around her in their brief time together.

'Are you a dream, now?' she asked, as her brain refused to provide any other answer to his sudden materialisation.

'I dropped on to the *Fan* when the helicopter came out to bring in the two fire-fighters who were burned,' he told her, while his eyes seemed to be relaying another message.

I love you, they seemed to be saying, but she was tired, and might be getting things wrong.

'The helicopter came from Craigstown!' she argued, pleased to find a fact she still knew.

'I flew up as soon as I heard about the fire,' he said, lowering her gently to the makeshift bed and squatting on the floor beside her as he drew a blanket over her shaking body. 'Made quite a fuss when I found I couldn't get out to the Bay!' he added reflectively, the wry smile that told her he was laughing at himself curling up one corner of his lips.

She reached out and touched his cheek, as if to reassure herself that he was real.

'Sleep now, my sweet Alice,' he said, pushing tendrils of hair back from her face with a touch that seemed to hint at love. 'We'll have plenty of time to talk later.'

* * *

The smoke was chokingly thick, blurring the edges of the room with a dull shadowing, but there was an air of excitement, of triumph even, charging the atmosphere as she sat up on the stretcher and tried to orientate her hazy mind and aching body.

Had Simon been a dream? Her eyes searched the people who milled around the room, then her conscience prodded her off the bed. There were people here who needed attention.

'The fire's been turned! The wind swung round enough for them to back-burn from the edge of town.' It was Mary Parsons, bearing a cup of tea and a plate of sandwiches. 'I made you fresh tea, seeing you went to sleep before you drank the last one.'

'How long ago?' Gemma asked, while her eyes searched the room on the off-chance that he hadn't been a dream.

'Four hours, you've had. It's not enough, but we're still getting a stream of casualties, and, as the ambulance has gone back out to bring in more, your doctor friend could probably do with a hand.'

He is here! she thought, feeling the flickering flames of excitement heating her tired body. Be sensible, a tiny part of her brain warned, so she sat where she was, ate the sandwiches and drank the tea, then ducked out to the washrooms to splash some water on her face and hands.

'Not a pretty sight,' she told her reflection, seeing the straggling hair and too pale skin, dusted with ash that only liberal amounts of soap and hot water would remove.

Then, somehow, it didn't matter, and she hurried back to the hall. Falling in beside the tall figure with a brief hello and a valiant smile, she began to cut away burnt clothing, to clean and soothe and wrap the wounds of the men and women who queued for help.

Now that the danger to the town had been averted, more men were leaving the line to come in for attention, suddenly feeling pain in wounds that they had not realised they had.

By lunchtime the road was cleared and a medical team from Craigstown had arrived to take over.

Gemma walked across to where Simon stood talking to one of the new arrivals. All the questions that work had kept at bay came flooding into her brain. Why had he come? Was he staying? What about Melbourne and his practice there? Had he walked out and left it, and, if so, why?

'We can go home now,' she said quietly, not knowing any answers and unwilling to ask the questions!

'Dave said he'd drive us if you're ready,' he responded, as naturally as if he had lived here all his life. He nodded farewell to the other doctor and slipped an arm around her shoulders as they walked towards the door.

'Shower and then bed,' he told her as they walked on to the veranda, black with ash from the burnt-out forest above the house. 'We'll talk later.'

With his hands on her shoulders, he propelled her towards the bathroom, and her unresisting body let him guide her all the way.

'Shall I shower you?' he asked, with such loving tenderness that she wanted to cry, but she shook her head. Her body was bombarded with the messages his conveyed so effortlessly, but a deadly weariness seemed to be dampening her responses, and the gritty feel of dirt and grime demanded privacy.

'Don't be long,' he murmured, dropping the lightest of kisses on her cracked lips.

Stripping off her clothes was completed in a matter of seconds, then, unbraiding her hair with fingers that shook like an old woman's, she turned on the water to a hot, steady stream and stepped under the shower, feeling the grit slowly slough away. Shampoo and soap restored a squeaky cleanliness to her hair and skin, and the warmth of the water relaxed tired muscles and eased aching bones.

She turned it off at last, and rubbed at her hair until all the surface moisture was absorbed by the thick towel. Slipping into her light summer robe, she hung a large dry towel over the rack for Simon, and left the room, hairdrier and brush clutched in her hands.

'Shower's free,' she called, embarrassed now by the unexpected intimacy of his presence in the house. What did she do next?

As no simple answer presented itself, she walked through to her bedroom, sat down on the bed, brushed out her hair, then turned on the drier to blow hot air through the thick skeins in an effort to dry it before she slept again.

Sleep! She'd been exhausted earlier, yet now her body was alive with exotic tensions that vibrated beneath the surface of her skin, and fizzed and sizzled in her blood.

When her arm began to ache with the strain of holding the brush, she bent forward on the bed, and let her hair fall forward, cascading to the ground like a honey-coloured curtain of gossamer-fine silk. She brushed downwards now, and blew the warm air through the strands, which dried quickly under her practised attention.

Then her body told her he was there, singing out to his with an urgent, demanding need. The brush was lifted from her fingers, and she snapped off the drier as he pushed the cloud of hair back from her face and knelt between her legs, his chest bare above the towel he had knotted round his waist. Smoothing back her hair with hands that trembled, he leaned forward to kiss her gently on the lips.

'Commitment is a word that's gained a lot of credence in my mind,' he told her, his lips moving against hers as he whispered his confession.

The taste of him made her shake with unleashed desire, and she reached out to touch his bare, satiny flesh, and feel the dancing pulses beneath his smooth, tanned skin.

'We should sleep first,' he murmured, but his hands were inside her robe, lifting her backwards to lie on the bed. Then his body was close above her as their skin sought to share the myriad sensations the magic that existed between them was producing.

Lips and fingers moved, seeking knowledge of each other's bodies that their minds already knew, finding all the secret places of delight that would enrich their shared experience to the point of ecstatic fulfilment.

Tiredness drained away as the urgency of their desire escalated. With her body fired to a burning hunger, Gemma met and matched his passion, dimly aware that the almost mystical quality of their bodies' response to each other was a very rare and precious delight.

Then all thought ceased as they came together and the rhythm of their movements slowed while they savoured the rightness of the new experience. Then her muscles claimed him and they moved together, into a place where time did not exist, as spangled lights and flashing stars lit realms of wonder beyond even the greatest of fairy-stories, and she was transported with him into another plane of existence.

'And I thought we were tired,' he mumbled against her shoulder as they lay entwined together a long time later. The mild self-derogation that tinged his words made her smile and hold him tighter. It was part of the appeal of this man who had stolen her heart—this potent mix of fantasy and charm.

'I'll move to Melbourne,' she murmured against the slick wetness of his chest, willing to take whatever he had to offer. The words were barely formed before she fell into a deep and dreamless sleep.

'I have dreamt of waking with your hair around me since that first night at the Fish Kettle.'

His warm breath in her ear set her heart fluttering again, and she opened her eyes to make sure he wasn't a dream.

'Why did you come?' she asked, wondering—hoping!

He raised himself on to one elbow, propping his head on his hand, and looked down into her questioning eyes.

'I'd begun to think you might be more than a passing fancy in my life when I made some tentative enquiries about the abandoned practice in Craigstown,' he said, the intentness in his eyes belying the light, mocking tone of his voice. 'Then, when I found myself seeking—and finding, mind you—a partner for my own practice, I began to wonder if it had anything to do with my dreams of a woodland sylph with wise eyes and a temper you would not believe!'

His hand reached out and touched her face, stroking away a strand of hair that had strayed across her temple.

Gemma held her breath, fearing that any movement, even a lifting of her chest, might break the magic spell that grasped them in its thrall.

'I heard about the fires,' he went on carefully, 'and knew your over-abundant sense of duty would have you in the thick of things. Suddenly, it was imperative to get to you, to see with my own eyes that you were safe. I left the new partner in charge and flew up to Craigstown. I'll have to go back, but not yet, and not for long!'

The huskiness of his voice as much as the words he was saying brought tears to Gemma's eyes, and she reached up to pull him down and hold him close.

'I love you, Gemma,' he murmured into her tangled hair. 'I love you and need you and want you——'

'For a brief affair?' she asked hoarsely, knowing she had to hear the words that had whispered in her heart.

'Only if it lasts forever,' he replied, and wrapped his arms around her as if he would never let her go.